The dri[illegible]
passen[illegible]
better

He hadn't been wearing a seat belt and when the car hit the cement pylon, he'd been slammed back into his seat with such force that he appeared to have broken his back. A SAR-21 still lay in his lap, but the man couldn't move his arms. Both his right arm and the right arm of the driver bore the distinctive question-mark tattoo with which the Executioner had become far too familiar over the past few days.

"Who sent you?" Bolan asked.

"The Malaysian," the man said just before he sunk into unconsciousness, confirming the soldier's suspicions. Bolan felt the pulse in the man's neck. He doubted the man was going to make it.

Bolan could hear sirens approaching in the distance. A delay would likely result in the deaths of hundreds of thousands of people, so the Executioner was on his motorcycle riding toward San Francisco before the first emergency vehicle came into sight. He held his speed to a reasonable level until after he'd passed the last squad car responding to the accident, then poured it on. He felt relatively sure he wouldn't get stopped for speeding since just about every available unit in a ten-mile area seemed to have headed for the accident site.

MACK BOLAN®
The Executioner

#303 Sea of Terror
#304 Soviet Specter
#305 Point Position
#306 Mercy Mission
#307 Hard Pursuit
#308 Into the Fire
#309 Flames of Fury
#310 Killing Heat
#311 Night of the Knives
#312 Death Gamble
#313 Lockdown
#314 Lethal Payload
#315 Agent of Peril
#316 Poison Justice
#317 Hour of Judgment
#318 Code of Resistance
#319 Entry Point
#320 Exit Code
#321 Suicide Highway
#322 Time Bomb
#323 Soft Target
#324 Terminal Zone
#325 Edge of Hell
#326 Blood Tide
#327 Serpent's Lair
#328 Triangle of Terror
#329 Hostile Crossing
#330 Dual Action
#331 Assault Force
#332 Slaughter House
#333 Aftershock
#334 Jungle Justice
#335 Blood Vector
#336 Homeland Terror
#337 Tropic Blast
#338 Nuclear Reaction
#339 Deadly Contact
#340 Splinter Cell
#341 Rebel Force
#342 Double Play
#343 Border War
#344 Primal Law
#345 Orange Alert
#346 Vigilante Run
#347 Dragon's Den
#348 Carnage Code
#349 Firestorm
#350 Volatile Agent
#351 Hell Night
#352 Killing Trade
#353 Black Death Reprise
#354 Ambush Force
#355 Outback Assault
#356 Defense Breach
#357 Extreme Justice
#358 Blood Toll
#359 Desperate Passage
#360 Mission to Burma
#361 Final Resort
#362 Patriot Acts
#363 Face of Terror
#364 Hostile Odds
#365 Collision Course
#366 Pele's Fire
#367 Loose Cannon
#368 Crisis Nation
#369 Dangerous Tides
#370 Dark Alliance
#371 Fire Zone
#372 Lethal Compound
#373 Code of Honor
#374 System Corruption
#375 Salvador Strike
#376 Frontier Fury
#377 Desperate Cargo
#378 Death Run

Don Pendleton's

The Executioner®

DEATH RUN

A GOLD EAGLE BOOK FROM
WORLDWIDE®

TORONTO • NEW YORK • LONDON
AMSTERDAM • PARIS • SYDNEY • HAMBURG
STOCKHOLM • ATHENS • TOKYO • MILAN
MADRID • WARSAW • BUDAPEST • AUCKLAND

First edition May 2010

ISBN-13: 978-0-373-64378-3

Special thanks and acknowledgment to
Darwin Holmstrom for his contribution to this work.

DEATH RUN

Printed in U.S.A.

He conquers who endures.

—Persius 34–62 A.D.

I will endure no matter what the odds against my success. It is the only way I know how to win.

—Mack Bolan

THE MACK BOLAN LEGEND

Nothing less than a war could have fashioned the destiny of the man called Mack Bolan. Bolan earned the Executioner title in the jungle hell of Vietnam.

But this soldier also wore another name—Sergeant Mercy. He was so tagged because of the compassion he showed to wounded comrades-in-arms and Vietnamese civilians.

Mack Bolan's second tour of duty ended prematurely when he was given emergency leave to return home and bury his family, victims of the Mob. Then he declared a one-man war against the Mafia.

He confronted the Families head-on from coast to coast, and soon a hope of victory began to appear. But Bolan had broken society's every rule. That same society started gunning for this elusive warrior—to no avail.

So Bolan was offered amnesty to work within the system against terrorism. This time, as an employee of Uncle Sam, Bolan became Colonel John Phoenix. With a command center at Stony Man Farm in Virginia, he and his new allies—Able Team and Phoenix Force—waged relentless war on a new adversary: the KGB.

But when his one true love, April Rose, died at the hands of the Soviet terror machine, Bolan severed all ties with Establishment authority.

Now, after a lengthy lone-wolf struggle and much soul-searching, the Executioner has agreed to enter an "arm's-length" alliance with his government once more, reserving the right to pursue personal missions in his Everlasting War.

Prologue

Losail Circuit, Doha, Qatar

Darrick Anderson rode onto the track for the first practice session of the MotoGP season, rolled on the throttle and felt the 800cc four-stroke V-four engine spin the cold rear tire like soft butter on hot bread. The adrenaline rush he always felt when he headed out on the track fueled his body for the grueling session ahead, heightening his senses and slowing his perception of time's passing. He leaned the bike into Turn One at a leisurely 110 miles per hour and shifted his body to the opposite side of the bike in preparation for the next corner.

The bike felt good, and he was grateful to have a position, even if it was on the Free Flow Racing team. Free Flow was a newcomer to motorcycle racing's premiere class. Like any new race team running machinery of its own design, it campaigned undeveloped and uncompetitive motorcycles. Anderson knew he'd be duking it out with the back markers instead of battling for victory at the front of the pack.

Beggars can't be choosers, he thought. It had only been five years since he'd had the number "one" painted on the fairing of his motorcycle. Throughout his career Anderson had battled not just the world's top motorcycle racers, but also his own addictions to alcohol and drugs. He'd usually won the on-track battles, and had three world championships to prove it, but he'd lost the battle to his addictions. His race performance became inconsistent, and at the age of twenty-five he found himself unable to find a place on a racing team in his native United States. Now Anderson had a second chance to prove himself, and he wanted to make the most of it.

No one expected Anderson to return to MotoGP racing—no one expected him to live long enough—but he'd cleaned up. He hadn't taken a drink or snorted a line of cocaine in almost two years. He'd gotten back in shape and regained his riding abilities. When he landed the Free Flow ride, his skills were at their peak, even if his bike was underpowered and its chassis underdeveloped.

As he brought his bike up to speed and warmed up his tires, none of this mattered; he was just happy to be out on the track, tearing it up with his brother Eddie under the hot desert sun.

Eddie Anderson rose through the ranks of motorcycle racing in the United States to become the youngest person ever to win a national Superbike championship. His performance earned the young phenomenon a spot on the Ducati Marlboro MotoGP team. After winning rookie of the year in his first season, Eddie had a good chance of taking the championship this season.

Darrick circled the track, knocking a few tenths of a second off his lap times with each revolution of the fast circuit. The machine beneath him felt good, better than he'd expected. He skimmed his knees on the apron as he apexed the last corner on the track, straightened the bike and exited hard onto the front straight. He nearly jumped off his saddle when he felt a hand slap his ass. Darrick looked out of the left side of his helmet and saw Eddie passing him. Darrick could keep up with Eddie in the corners, but Eddie's powerful bike ran away from Darrick's as they rode down the long front straight. Eddie gained several bike lengths on Darrick before he threw his bike into Turn One.

There was a time when being passed would have thrown Darrick into spasms of rage, but seeing Eddie ride, watching him display his amazing skill and grace, made Darrick smile. He looked forward to his brother taking the number-one plate. Darrick pushed his bike to its very limits and beyond, not because he wanted to beat Eddie, but because he wanted to keep his brother in sight and watch him ride.

Darrick did a good job keeping up with his hard-charging brother, but the harder he pushed, the worse his bike behaved. The front end started to chatter under braking and continued to get worse until the bike was nearly in a tank slapper, forcing him into the paddock to have his technicians sort out the suspension. He pulled into the Free Flow pit, handed his bike to one of the technicians, peeled the top of his one-piece leathers to his waist, and went into the garage to find his team manager and explain the suspension problem. It would probably take only minor adjustments to dial out the front-end chatter and he wanted to get back out on the track before the two-hour practice session ended. He knew there was little point in trying to communicate the problem to the non-English-speaking technician.

It was early Friday morning and the paddock was quiet. The other racers were just starting to trickle out on the track, and a few teams hadn't even completely set up in their garages yet. Within the hour the sleepy paddock would transform into a buzzing industrial worksite. It would remain so until long after the traffic jam that would inevitably followed Sunday's race dissipated.

Darrick walked through the garage toward the office to find Jameed Botros, his team manager. He hated to complain because he didn't want anyone to think he'd fallen back into his prima donna ways, but Botros always set him on edge. There was something wrong with the man, and with the entire Free Flow team itself.

Free Flow, a Malaysian motorcycle company that specialized in building scooters and small motorcycles for Third World markets, had begun developing larger motorcycles for the lucrative U.S. and European markets. Free Flow's MotoGP race team was part of an effort to build brand recognition in those markets. Though the team was headquartered in Malaysia, most of the technicians and mechanics were Saudis, and none of them spoke English except Botros. Given that the Free Flow team's primary sponsor was a Saudi oil company, it made sense that the team was composed exclusively of Saudis.

It didn't bother Darrick that they were Saudis; what bothered him was that they were hard men who seemed out of place in the MotoGP world. They didn't seem to like motorcycles or motorcycle racing all that much. They didn't seem to like much else, either, especially Darrick. He'd never worked with such grim, humorless men.

Darrick walked into the office to find Botros speaking with a uniformed member of the Qatar security force. Because of the background noise from the activity in the garage, Botros and the security officer didn't notice Darrick enter the room. Botros continued to speak to the man in Arabic. Darrick had picked up enough of the language to recognize the words *package* and *shipment.* He also made out the English names *San Francisco* and *Mazda Raceway* in the snippet of conversation he overheard. The fact that Botros was discussing the following week's race at the Mazda Raceway near Monterey, California, with a member of the Qatar security force struck Darrick as odd, and his face betrayed his concern.

Darrick said, "*Samehni,*" Arabic for "pardon me," one of the phrases he'd picked up. Botros glared at him and said nothing. Darrick switched to English and explained the front-end chatter to Botros, who promised to have a technician make the changes Darrick suggested.

Darrick retired to his motor home to freshen up while the bike was being prepared. When he returned to the garage for the last part of the morning practice session, a particularly humorless technician, a Saudi Darrick hadn't met before, had his bike running and ready to go out on track. With his heavily scarred face, the man looked more like an escapee from a harsh prison than a trained motorcycle mechanic. "Your motorcycle is ready, sir," the man said.

Astonished to hear the brutish man speak English, Darrick thanked him, then donned his helmet and gloves and rode out of the garage. He got out on track just as Eddie flew by at full throttle. Darrick knew he should let his tires warm up a bit, but he couldn't resist the urge to chase his brother. He accelerated hard down the front straight, sat up to get into position for the first turn, and grabbed a handful of brake. Instead of pushing the brake pads into the discs, the brake lever went soft and pulled all the way back to the clip-on handlebar. A mist of brake fluid shot up inside his helmet, numbing his lips and stinging his eyes. His brake line had come loose from the reservoir on the handlebar. Riding nearly two hundred miles per hour into Turn One, he had no brakes.

Darrick leaned the bike into the turn and the front wheel

lost traction, throwing the motorcycle to the pavement, shattering Darrick's collarbone. He skidded off the track alongside the motorcycle and hit the gravel at the outside apex of the turn. In most crashes his protective gear would save him from serious injury, but no gear on Earth would help him if he hit the wall at that speed.

He tried to slow himself, but when he saw the clip-on handlebar of the motorcycle dig into the gravel and launch the machine skyward, he knew it no longer mattered. The bike flew twenty feet in the air and Darrick watched as it started to come down at him. He tried to roll onto his side even though he knew it would make him go airborne and flop around like a rag doll in a tornado. As he expected, his broken shoulder caught in the gravel and flipped him over, launching him feet first into the air. Before he could make an entire revolution, which would have jammed his head into the gravel and snapped his neck, the motorcycle came down across his chest. Man and machine hit the wall as one, crushing the life from Darrick's body. His last thought before impact was that he was never going to see his brother win the MotoGP championship.

Mack Bolan crouched behind the cargo container in the Doha Industrial Area, watching the Qatar security force officer walk past on his rounds. Bolan had timed the man's route and knew he had just short of thirty minutes to examine the shipping containers that had been transferred from the Pakistani container ship *Hammam.*

The previous night the soldier had slipped aboard the ship while it was anchored in the Doha Port and located the containers identified as his targets. He hadn't had time to examine the containers, which were covered in blue tarps. However, he managed to place an electronic tracking device under one of the tarps before he had to clear off the ship.

That morning, he'd followed the trucks hauling the ship's cargo to the warehouse. He'd located the cargo containers with a hand-held tracking unit disguised as a cellular phone and followed the signal to the corner of the warehouse. The crates were still covered with blue tarps.

When the security officer left the warehouse, the Executioner unfastened the tie-downs securing the blue tarp and pulled the back corner aside, revealing a rear hatch locked down tight by a high-security hardened steel padlock with a hardened steel shackle. It would take more than his .44 Magnum Desert Eagle to blast through that lock, but it didn't matter. He couldn't use a gun in the warehouse without alerting the guard, not even his sound-suppressed Beretta 93-R.

Bolan pulled the blue tarp back to reveal a red-and-yellow paint scheme. A painting of a blue racing motorcycle adorned the side of the container. He pulled the tarp farther back to reveal the words Free Flow Racing emblazoned on the bike's fairing. It wasn't what the soldier expected to see. According to the intel he'd received from Aaron "the Bear" Kurtzman, these containers held the ten kilograms of weapon-grade plutonium that disappeared in Pakistan the previous week. That was enough of the dense substance to build a nuclear bomb capable of destroying an entire city.

The president of the United States had ordered Hal Brognola, Director of the Justice Department's Special Operations Group, to get the plutonium back. Because sources indicated that the material had gone to Qatar, getting it back would be a delicate task, given the close relationship between Qatar and the United States. Qatar, an independent emirate that jutted into the Persian Gulf—or *Arab Gulf,* as the locals called it—was one of the few remaining countries in the Middle East that welcomed U.S. military bases. Though the tiny emirate was politically stable thanks to its oil wealth, Qatar's relatively moderate policies—it had been the first Arab nation to allow women to vote—made it a target for fanatical Islamic fundamentalists. The emir didn't want to agitate the region's radical factions by allowing the U.S. military to conduct an overt operation to retrieve the stolen plutonium so the Man asked Brognola to send in a discrete force. The big Fed assigned the task to the force of one known as the Executioner.

Because plutonium 239 is extremely toxic when inhaled or ingested—absorbing only a few micrograms causes cancer—

destroying the ship would have been the equivalent of setting off a massive dirty bomb in the Doha Port, killing thousands of innocent Qatarians. Bolan had to find the material himself. He knew his job wouldn't be easy. Though one of the most toxic substances ever created, plutonium 239 emits very little gamma radiation, making it virtually undetectable.

Because it ignites at room temperature when exposed to oxygen, plutonium 239 needs to be transported in a self-cooling container. Kurtzman discovered that a German firm had recently built an unusual type B container—a ductile iron cask with plumbing for coolant, a shock absorbing outer casing, and a nickel-lined interior coated with a synthetic resin that sealed in all radiation—that was small enough to fit in the back of a cargo van. The container had been shipped to a client in Pakistan. The only possible use for such a container would be the transport of nuclear material. When Kurtzman investigated the client, supposedly a Chinese energy research company, it turned out to be nothing more than a post office box in Grand Cayman.

The same source that alerted U.S. intelligence to the theft of the plutonium believed the material had been transported to the Port of Karachi, where it would be shipped to Qatar. The Bear's team hit their computers and tracked every cargo shipment leaving Pakistan for Qatar. The manifest of one vessel, the container ship *Hammam,* contained anomalies that caught the attention of Stony Man's cyberdetectives, convincing Kurtzman that this was their ship. Now Bolan stood before the containers that the team had identified.

The Executioner didn't hear anything behind him but suddenly sensed the pair of eyes boring into him from behind. Instinctively, he threw himself forward and rolled over on his shoulder to see the security officer lining him up in the sights of a Heckler & Koch MP-5. Bolan flattened himself against the concrete floor and felt the initial volley of bullets skim over the top of his head. As the security guard fired, the muzzle rise made his trajectory climb, giving Bolan room to scramble behind the container.

If he'd been going up against an outlaw or terrorist, Bolan would have simply killed the man shooting at him. But the Executioner didn't want to kill law enforcement officers, whether they were U.S. cops or members of Qatar's national security force. He'd have to find another way out of this predicament, one that didn't involve using his own guns.

He pushed his foot into the blue canvas and gained a foothold on one of the metal support ribs that ran the length of the cargo container. With a kick, he propelled himself high enough to grab the top of the container, and with the grace of a gymnast, he swung himself onto the top of the container. Because the security officer had still been firing his weapon, he hadn't heard Bolan land atop the container.

When the shooting stopped, Bolan raised his head just enough to catch a glimpse of the officer. The greasepaint on the soldier's face made him hard to see in the dark warehouse, but his blacksuit wasn't providing much camouflage against the blue tarp. Bolan watched the officer creep toward the wall, where he could see behind the container. When he looked up, he'd see Bolan on top of it. The soldier grabbed an M-84 flashbang grenade from the vest he wore over his blacksuit, pulled the pin and lobbed the grenade over the edge of the container toward the officer.

The man spotted the motion and fired at Bolan. He only

got off one round before the flashbang detonated, but that round struck the soldier square in the chest. He wore a vest containing an experimental lightweight armor that John "Cowboy" Kissinger had developed back at Stony Man Farm. The weapons specialist claimed this thin, flexible armor could stop anything up to and including a standard 7.62 mm round, though he wasn't sure about high-velocity armor-piercing rounds. Fortunately it was capable of stopping the 9 mm round from the officer's machine pistol, though the bullet struck the Executioner with enough force to knock him over the edge of the container.

Still in midair when the flashbang went off, Bolan covered his ears, closed his eyes and let out a shriek to equalize the pressure in his lungs. He landed on his feet, his legs pumping as soon as they hit the ground. The security officer would recover from the flashbang, but not before Bolan slipped back into the vent through which he'd entered the building.

Doha was a quiet city, and if the shots that the officer fired didn't bring nearly all eight thousand men of the Qatar security force to the warehouse, the flashbang's explosion certainly would.

The Executioner moved the grate covering the vent pipe aside, slid inside, replaced the grate and climbed up the pipe. When he got to the top of the vent, he crawled through the rectangular vent pipe that ran along the roof toward a blower fan until he reached the hole he'd cut in the bottom of the pipe. There was only about eighteen inches between the pipe and the roof of the warehouse so he had to snake his way out of the pipe. He could see flashing blue lights from the security force vehicles driving toward the front of the warehouse. Bolan ran to the back edge of the roof where he'd left the rope he'd used to climb up and clipped his descender to the rope. He let himself down the side of the building as fast as he could without breaking any bones. Upon hitting the ground, he ran toward the hole he'd cut in the security fence on his way into the warehouse facility. He was in his Range Rover and driving back toward his hotel before the security officers even discovered he'd left the building.

Bolan was grateful that he hadn't injured any of the officers who kept the peace in the tiny emirate. Qatar's security force had a reputation for being good cops, honest and reasonable men who had never been charged with a human rights violation.

He hadn't been so lucky; he was pretty sure he'd broken a rib when he took the round from the officer's MP-5, but he'd survive. He hadn't located the plutonium, but at least he had a lead: Free Flow Racing. He knew that the Losail circuit in Doha would be hosting Grand Prix motorcycle races that weekend. He wouldn't be able to get back in the warehouse after the fiasco that had just occurred, but at least he knew where to look.

First, he'd have to find a reason to be at the race. He drove back to his hotel and dialed the secure number for Stony Man Farm on his cell phone. It took a few moments for the signal to travel its circuitous but untraceable route before he heard Kurtzman on the line. "What's up, Striker?" Kurtzman asked, using Bolan's Stony Man code name.

"I need to be someone else," Bolan replied.

"Anyone in particular?"

"I'd kind of like to try an average Joe, but maybe another time. Right now I need to be a salesman."

POSING AS MATT COOPER, Bolan presented his credentials to the paddock guard. Overnight Kurtzman had created a background for Cooper, an American sales rep for the racing fuels division of CCP Petroleum, a Russian company created from the ashes of the failed Yukos Oil. Cooper's assignment was to get MotoGP racing teams to use CCP racing fuel. To create the character of Cooper, Bolan, who spoke decent Russian, spent the night studying the recent history of Grand Prix motorcycle racing.

The Fédération Internationale de Motocyclisme (FIM) formed the MotoGP class, motorcycle racing's most prestigious racing series, for the 2002 season. Originally FIM had dictated that 990 cc four-strokes raced in the class. When those motorcycles became so powerful that their performance outpaced the limits of tire technology, the FIM lowered the displacement limit to 800 cc for the 2007 racing season.

Darrick Anderson, an American rider, dominated the first three seasons of MotoGP, but problems with alcohol and other drugs had destroyed his career. He'd disappeared for several years, but this year he was back. Bolan had Darrick's name at the top of the list of people he planned to interview, since Darrick was Free Flow Racing's top rider.

Posing as Cooper's assistant at CCP's American branch, Barbara Price, Stony Man's mission controller, had arranged meetings with representatives from several MotoGP teams. Most top teams were already supported by major oil companies so the story was that CCP targeted smaller teams. Since MotoGP teams didn't get any smaller than Free Flow Racing, it only made sense that Cooper would meet with them first. Price set up a meeting with Team Free Flow Racing's general manager Jameed Botros.

Bolan arrived at the Free Flow Racing garage complex in the Losail paddock fifteen minutes before his scheduled meeting with Mr. Botros but found the area deserted. The doors were open, so he let himself inside, hoping to find out where everyone was, but the garages were empty. The Executioner walked toward a wall covered with television monitors and realized why the complex was empty. From several different angles the monitors showed Darrick Anderson's lifeless body being loaded onto a helicopter. Bolan could tell things didn't look good for Mr. Anderson.

He looked around the building and saw several containers identical to the ones he'd seen in the warehouse the previous night. He activated the GPS locator in his cell phone and saw that the container he wanted had to be either in the very back of the garage complex or behind it. He made his way to the rear of the complex without finding the container.

He punched a button that opened one of the overhead doors in the back wall and went outside, where he found the container he'd tagged with the homing device still secured to the bed of a truck trailer. He examined it and saw that the seals applied to the container in Pakistan still hadn't been broken.

Bolan turned around and found himself face-to-face with a man dressed as a member of the Qatar security force, though the dagger in his hand was not standard-issue for the force. Bolan hadn't heard the man approach because of the noise generated by the barely muffled motorcycle engines that permeated the entire Losail facility. The officer lunged at Bolan with the dagger, its tip contacting Bolan's rib cage just below his left armpit. Because the Executioner had moved back the moment he saw the blade coming at him, the dagger barely penetrated his skin.

Bolan brought his left elbow down on the attacker's arm, snapping both the radius and ulna bones in his forearm. The man fell beneath the force of the blow. Bolan reached around with his right hand and caught the knife as it fell from the attacker's disabled hand. The man lunged forward and in an instinctive reaction Bolan sliced upward with the knife, catching the man several inches below the navel and cutting all the way up to his rib cage.

The man staggered backward and fell, clutching his midsection in a failed attempt to hold in the intestines that poured from his eviscerated abdomen. Bolan knew this man most likely was not a cop. Cops didn't try to assassinate strangers with daggers, especially Qatar's security force officers. He was certain that the man he'd just gutted was a criminal posing as a security officer.

Bolan pulled his Beretta from his shoulder holster and asked the man, who was dying too slowly to avoid intense suffering, "Do you speak English?" He received no answer. The man had entered a state of shock and wasn't able to respond. Bolan estimated he would be dead within minutes.

He holstered the Beretta and began searching the body for some identification but stopped when he heard movement behind him. He spun around just in time to see a steel pipe swinging toward his temple. Then the lights went out.

The Persian Gulf

The Executioner knew he was on a boat the moment he regained consciousness. From the sound of the muffled diesel engines and the carpeted floor on which he lay, he guessed he was on some sort of pleasure craft. The musty smell of the carpet told him it was an older boat. He heard at least two people conversing in Arabic, but otherwise he deduced very little information about his current situation. What felt like duct tape covered his eyes and mouth. His hands were bound behind his back and his feet were tied together tight, presumably with the same material.

His head hurt almost as much as his broken rib, but the soldier suffered in silence. He didn't want his captors to know he was awake. Though he didn't speak Arabic, he'd picked up some phrases here and there and was able to glean some information about his captors, most importantly that they were Saudis, not Qatarians.

They were angry Saudis. Apparently the man that Bolan had sent to visit Allah back at the racetrack had been one of their brethren. This virtually eliminated the possibility that he'd killed a law enforcement officer, since Bolan knew Qatar didn't hire Saudis for its police force. Qatar had a dark side when it came to its discrimination against immigrants, especially Saudis, because of the poor relationship Qatar had with its giant neighbor to the west. The two countries had only recently settled a border dispute that had simmered for almost two decades.

Bolan could hear the sound of other boats over the angry conversation between the Saudis. Because he couldn't hear the telltale industrial noise of the Doha Port, he guessed that he was either in the Doha Harbor or the Old Harbor area. As he listened, the sound of the other boats grew more distant, which meant they were leaving the harbor and heading out to open water. Bolan didn't know how long he'd been out, but he guessed that it was no longer than an hour, and probably less.

Bolan lay immobile until the Saudis began to kick at him, gently prodding him at first, but getting progressively harder.

"Wake up!" one of the men shouted in English.

Bolan felt the duct tape rip away from his eyes, taking half his eyebrows with it.

"You're not dead yet!" The man ripped the tape away from Bolan's mouth with the same force he'd used to remove it from his eyes.

Bolan looked around the cabin of what seemed to be a sport fishing boat and estimated the craft to be thirty-five to forty feet in length. Looking out the cabin windows, he saw land on the starboard side, which meant that they were heading south.

In addition to the man who'd waxed the soldier's eyebrows with duct tape, two other men sat on a threadbare lounge, looking down at him. An AK-74 rested on each of their laps. The scar-faced thug who'd removed the duct tape wore the desert-camo uniform of a Qatar security force officer, but the AKSU-74 machine pistol slung around his neck and shoulder indicated he was an imposter—the well-funded Qatarian forces carried top-shelf European weapons, not twenty-year-old Russian sub machine guns.

The man whose patchwork face looked like it had been launched through a dozen windshields, grabbed Bolan and hoisted him up onto a stool by the galley counter. The two goons took a roll of duct tape and taped Bolan's ankles to the stool's pedestal, then gave his wrists another round of tape, tightening up the soldier's bonds. This put him in an awkward position; it took all his effort to remain upright on the stool, leaving him completely vulnerable.

"So tell me Mr. Cooper," the scarred man said in heavily accented English, "Why are you such a curious gas peddler? What were you doing with this?" He held up the satellite tracking device the soldier had attached to the shipping container. Before Bolan could say anything, the man backhanded him across his face, nearly knocking him off the stool. He felt his nasal cavity fill with blood.

When Bolan righted himself on the stool, the man put the barrel of his AKSU against the soldier's forehead. Unable to move his hands, Bolan realized that his war everlasting might finally be about to reach its end. The Saudi slowly squeezed the trigger. The Russian Kalashnikovs weren't known for their clean trigger breaks and time seemed to stop as Bolan watched the man slowly squeeze. Though it was barely perceptible, he saw the man's finger tense up as the sear hit the breaking point.

Instead of the muzzle blast he expected, Bolan only heard the firing pin click on an empty chamber. All three men laughed.

"You should be so lucky," the man said. "Death is preferable to the fate my boss has in store for you. We have to keep you alive for two more days. When my boss comes, he'll send you to hell long before you have the good fortune to die."

"Who's your boss?" Bolan asked.

Instead of replying, the man smashed the machine pistol into the side of Bolan's head, once again knocking him unconscious.

2

Jameed Botros hated racing. He hated motorcycles and he hated the people who rode them. He had never cared for any form of Western decadence, but being in the center of one of the West's biggest and gaudiest spectacles was almost too much for him to bear. The only thing that kept him going was the fact that he hated the Western world even more than he hated motorcycle racing. And if all went as planned, this would be a very short racing season.

So far everything had been going as planned, until that damned gasoline sales rep had showed up and started nosing around. Somehow he had known which container held the plutonium. If he knew, surely others knew, which meant that they would have to get their equipment to America fast, and once there, they would have to alter all their plans.

Botros' boss, Musa bin Osman, Free Flow's vice president in charge of all racing activities, had chastised him for killing the American racer. Botros knew he might well have met a worse fate than Darrick Anderson's had he not convinced his superior that the American had overheard him discussing the plan with Nasir, his compatriot who was posing as a member of the Qatar security force.

Nasir had the troublesome sales rep trapped aboard a fishing boat. Botros had wanted to kill the big stranger immediately, but bin Osman wanted to interrogate him before killing him. He wanted to know exactly what this man knew, or thought he'd known, about their operation. He wanted to find out who the big man really worked for, how he and his employers learned of the plutonium, and how much they knew about Team Free Flow's planned activities in the U.S. As bin Osman wanted to question the man himself, but he couldn't arrive until Sunday, the day of the race, Botros and his men had been forced to keep the interloper alive.

Botros thought the Malaysian businessman was making a mistake by keeping the man alive. The big American was clearly a man to be reckoned with. He had dispatched with one of Botros' best men as if squashing an ant. Bin Osman is weak, he thought. He is as much a slave to his own vices as any Westerner. In this case, bin Osman's vice was the thrill he received from torturing a human being to death. Botros had watched him do it on several occasions, and the pleasure bin Osman received from the act seemed almost of a sexual nature. Botros found his boss's behavior disgusting, but he didn't dare call him on it lest bin Osman decide that Botros himself might make a fitting subject on which to practice his fetish.

Botros had come close to finding out what it would be like to be tortured at the hands of his superior after he had killed Darrick Anderson, but he had placated bin Osman. Of course he had lied to the man; he had been looking for an excuse to kill the decadent young American since he first met him. Anderson, a drug addict, alcoholic and whoremonger, represented everything he hated about Westerners. Anderson claimed to have reformed, but Botros knew he only pretended to have given up his vices in order to attain a job racing motorcycles. He was still a weak American, a slave to his vices, and Botros knew that at the first opportunity he would return to his hedonistic ways. Botros had made a promise to Allah that he would kill Anderson at the first possible opportunity. Bin Osman, being a slave to his own vices, could not have understood why Botros had to do what he did.

But at least bin Osman shared Botros' hatred of Westerners. The Malaysian hadn't always been such a devout believer in *Wahhabism,* the ultraconservative form of Islam embraced by Osama bin Laden and al Qaeda, but his years of dealing with the West had converted him. As a young man, bin Osman had suckled at the teat of Western decadence, attending the finest universities in England and America, denying himself no pleasures of the flesh in the process.

But after a series of failed business ventures, the Malaysian had finally been made to see the need for *jihad* to cleanse the world of the social disease that was Western culture. At last bin Osman understood that the only way to bring that about was to have a world governed by *Sharia* law.

When the Malaysian allied himself with al Qaeda, he proved to be one of the most capable operatives the organization ever had. Now he was about to execute what would be not just a blow against the decadent West, but a death blow to Arab leaders who weakened *Sharia* with Western concepts. When bin Osman's plan came to fruition, there would be no so-called "moderate" Islamic states left, and the entire world would be subject to the strictest interpretations of *Sharia.*

Bin Osman may have still had his vices, but he also had the power to make Botros' desire a reality. He'd obtained the plutonium, he had the resources to make a bomb, and he had the connections needed to carry out the plan once they got to America. Botros may have hated the man, but he needed him more than he hated him.

WHEN BOLAN regained consciousness, he had no idea where he was. He could tell he was still on a boat, but the boat wasn't moving. *It took a few moments for him to remember Scarface striking him.* He had no idea what time it was, but the stiffness in his shoulders and legs told him he'd been out for a long time. He raised his head to look around and almost lost consciousness again. He realized he must have received a concussion from his captor's blow.

Through sheer force of will, the soldier made himself sit up and try to focus on his surroundings. He saw that he was in the lower bunk of a small stateroom. His hands were still bound behind his back and his ankles were still bound together, but at least they hadn't put duct tape over his eyes and mouth again.

He worked his way to the edge of the bunk, swung his legs over the edge, and stood, balancing on his tied-together legs as if they were a single limb. The small room had a sliding pocket door that probably led to the hallway between the main stateroom and the steps leading up to the galley. He looked out over the top bunk. From the angle of the light coming through the small rectangular window above the bunk, he could see that the sun was just starting to rise over the Persian Gulf. That meant that he'd been unconscious all night.

He looked around for anything he could use to help him escape from his bonds and spotted a nail that was working itself loose from the wood frame of the top bunk. The head of the nail rose just barely high enough above the wood for the Executioner to see a faint shadow around its edge. It might be enough.

Bolan put his mouth over the nail and worked it loose from the wood with his teeth. When he finally got it in his mouth, he bent down and spit it onto the mattress of the lower bunk, right where he estimated his hands might rest. Then he lay down on top of the bunk and felt the nail with his right hand. He grabbed the nail with his fingers and worked it around until the point was aimed at his wrists. Then with the heel of his hand he maneuvered the point of the nail under the edge of the duct tape. He pushed on the nail and felt the tape give just a little bit. He repeated the process and pushed the nail through a bit more of the tape. He repeated the maneuver over and over throughout the day, stopping only when he heard one of his captors coming to check on him. By the time night fell, he'd worked through almost an inch of the tape, not quite enough to break his hands free. He kept at it and by the time he worked his hands free, the sky was beginning to lighten again in the east.

When Bolan regained feeling in his extremities, he tested the sliding door to see if it made noise. It did, but its squeaks weren't any louder than the rest of the creaking emitted from the old boat as it rode the waves and he slid it open as quietly as possible. He stuck his head out the door and scanned the boat. To his right he saw the door to what must have been the forward stateroom. To his left he saw the steps leading up to the galley, and across from his stateroom he saw the open door to the bathroom.

He could hear loud snoring coming from the forward stateroom. Odds were that was where his lead captor slept, and the soldier wanted to keep him alive for questioning.

Softer snoring wafted from the salon area beyond the galley. Bolan crept up into the galley and looked over the counter to see one man sleeping on the lounge and another curled up on a smaller settee. The man on the lounge had been one of the men who had kicked him earlier; he didn't recognize the man on the settee. He couldn't see anyone out on the deck, but he heard movement on the flybridge above the cabin.

The Executioner knew he needed a weapon. He'd have to get one without alerting the man on the bridge or the man sleeping in the forward stateroom.

He looked around and saw a wooden block on the galley counter that held several knives. He pulled out a chef's knife, but the blade was so dull that the handle would have made a better weapon. The second knife he pulled out was a boning knife with a razor-sharp blade.

Bolan crept into the salon. The man sleeping on the lounge stirred and Bolan was forced to quickly slit his throat. The man died silently. Knowing what was at stake, Bolan had dispatched the second man in similar fashion.

The Executioner grabbed the second man's AK-74 and slung it over his shoulder, but kept his hand on the knife as he made his way to the ladder leading up to the flybridge. He crept up the ladder and peeked over the top. No one was at the helm, but the other man who had kicked him when he was first taken captive sat on a bench alongside the helm, looking toward land through a pair of binoculars. Bolan managed to get up on the flybridge and creep close to the helm before the man started to put down the binoculars.

Bolan rushed toward the man and before he could put down the binoculars and snatch his gun, the soldier plunged the knife blade into the side of the man's chest, just below the armpit. The seven-inch blade severed the man's main artery and he bled out before his heart beat five times.

A pool of the man's blood covered the floor of the flybridge and drops followed the soldier down the ladder to the deck, where they mixed with the water that had splashed on deck during the night. Inside the salon, pools of blood covered the upholstery of the lounge and settee, dripping off and soaking into the carpet below. Bolan walked past the bodies and went to the master stateroom. He threw the door open and fired the AK into the ceiling above the bed. Shards of fiberglass rained down on the leader's sleeping form.

The man lunged as Bolan had expected. What he didn't expect was that he would have a Glock pistol in his hand. The scarred man swung the weapon around toward the soldier, but before he could get the muzzle pointed in Bolan's direction, Bolan fired off several rounds into the man's face. In a split second his scars vanished, along with the rest of his features. And any hope the Executioner had of interrogating the man disappeared with his face.

3

Monterey, California

"There's no way in hell that Darrick's crash was an accident," Eddie Anderson told Matt Cooper, the sales rep for a Russian oil company. Anderson didn't question why a gasoline salesman was asking him about his late brother—he'd told everyone he talked to that he thought that his brother had been murdered. Most people wrote it off as the petulant outbursts of a young man in the throes of grief. But grief and anger didn't hamper his on-track performance; if anything, they enhanced it. Anderson won the race in Qatar by a huge margin, beating his teammate—the current champion, a hotheaded Spaniard named Daniel Asnorossa—by seven seconds.

Asnorossa earned his championship the previous year mostly because Anderson had crashed several times and had failed to finish three races while Asnorossa finished every race among the top five riders. Anderson won four races—three more than Asnorossa—and earned the rookie-of-the-year award. He'd been hired as Asnorossa's backup rider, but this year everyone treated the upstart American like the team's top rider.

Bolan missed Anderson's victory. He hadn't been able to get to the track before the entire MotoGP circus packed up and shipped off to the United States for the following weekend's race at Laguna Seca. After searching his captors' bodies, which turned up nothing but fake Qatar security force IDs, along with paddock passes for the Losail circuit, he'd ditched them in the Persian Gulf.

He hadn't been able to steam into one of Doha's heavily patrolled harbors in a blood-soaked boat registered to God knows who, especially with his light skin that immediately identified him as a Westerner. Qatarians didn't trust foreigners, and he would have been sure to attract attention of the official variety. He waited until nightfall, then abandoned the boat and swam to a relatively deserted beach. In the meantime he avoided attention by doing what anyone aboard a sport fishing boat would do when out on the water—he fished. There was nothing else he could do because the Arabs had taken all of his electronic equipment, including his cell phone, along with all of his weapons and ID.

After hitting shore he made his way back to his hotel room, where he was finally able to contact Stony Man Farm on a secure line. By the time he'd contacted Kurtzman, it was too late to stop the plane carrying the Team Free Flow equipment, which had already been offloaded and was en route to the Mazda Raceway.

By the time Hal Brognola could organize a raid on the Laguna Seca paddock, the plutonium would almost certainly have been removed from the container. Bolan only hoped it hadn't already been used to make a bomb.

While Stony Man's top pilot, Jack Grimaldi, flew Bolan to the Monterey Peninsula Airport, Kurtzman sent Bolan new information regarding the Free Flow Racing organization. Apparently things weren't going so well for the Malaysian scooter manufacturer. The costs of developing a full-sized motorcycle for the U.S. and European markets exceeded everyone's expectations and Free Flow was in a state of chaos, with a revolving roster of top executives, none of whom seem to survive even a year within the organization.

The one person who seemed to float above the turmoil was Musa bin Osman, Free Flow's vice president in charge of racing. That was in part because the racing organization was one of the few departments at Free Flow earning money, thanks to the generous sponsorship of a Saudi oil company. That was where things got interesting. The oil company was suspected of being a front for laundering money for several al Qaeda affiliates. The deeper Kurtzman dug, the more terrorist ties he discovered. Musa bin Osman had studied under the suspected mastermind behind the 2005 Bali bombings and many other terrorist attacks. He seemed to have close ties with Jemaah Islamiyah, the most active al Qaeda affiliate group in Malaysia.

Bolan knew that his Matt Cooper identity had likely been compromised, at least as far as the Team Free Flow organization was concerned, but it was still his quickest way to gain access to the racing paddock so he continued to play the role of a fuel sales rep for a Russian oil company. He had Barbara Price try to make an appointment to meet with Jameed Botros before he'd even landed at Monterey, but the earliest he could see the Saudi would be Thursday. In the meantime he scoped out the area around Laguna Seca.

To keep up appearances, he met with a couple of reps from satellite race teams—teams that leased the previous year's factory race bikes. Such teams had some factory support—some more than others—but mostly they fended for themselves and were hungry for any sponsorship. By Thursday Cooper had tentative agreements with two teams. More importantly, he'd picked up on an undercurrent of mistrust between Team Free Flow and the other MotoGP organizations.

On Thursday Bolan rode the BMW R1200GS he'd rented in San Francisco to the Free Flow garage to keep his appointment with Botros. The entire San Francisco area became an orgy of motorcycle activity during the week of the big race, and there was no better way for the soldier to blend in than to ride a motorcycle. Plus motorcycles were far more effective at slicing through the dense traffic that descended on the area for the race.

He'd chosen the BMW because it was one of the most agile motorcycles ever built. The big bike was too heavy for serious off-road work. But in the hands of a physically large rider like Bolan, it could scoot down some pretty rough trails if it had to. Bolan had ridden just about every motorcycle built since he began his vigilante war against the Mafia many years ago, and he'd also received training from some of the world's best on- and off-road motorcycle racers over the years, so he knew how to muscle a big bike over rough terrain.

The Executioner knew damned well that he was being set up, that if this meeting wasn't a trap, at the very least it would be the prelude to a trap. Botros and his crew might not try to kill him in the garage complex. They might keep a low profile at the track and attack Bolan somewhere off site. Or they might just try to kill him in their garages. But the soldier had made a commitment to recover the stolen plutonium before the terrorists had the chance to use it, and getting closer to the Team Free Flow crew, the only people who knew for sure where the plutonium was located, was the best way he could think of to find it.

Bolan knew that someone could try to kill him at any

moment. The soldier had no way of knowing where or when that attempt would take place so he'd have to rely on years of experience and instincts honed to an almost preternatural degree to survive the next few days. That, and the .44 Magnum Desert Eagle on his hip and the Beretta 93-R machine pistol he carried in the shoulder rig beneath his jacket.

Bolan parked the BMW near the Team Free Flow garages just in time to see Eddie Anderson being escorted from the building complex by a couple of Middle Eastern-looking men. One could have been Scarface's brother, or at least his cousin. The Arabs weren't having an easy time of it. Most successful motorcycle racers were built like jockeys, and Anderson was no exception; he stood maybe five-four in his racing boots and couldn't have weighed much, but he was giving the two Arabs as good as he got.

"Get your damned hands off of me!" Anderson told Scarface's cousin. "I know he was murdered and I know you guys did it!" The man tried to push Anderson to the ground but the wiry little rider ducked and grabbed the man's wrist, flipped his arm around behind his back, and pushed him face first into the tarmac. The other Arab grabbed Anderson before he could pounce on the fallen man and flung him into Bolan.

"Are you all right?" Bolan asked. Without answering, Anderson spun around to face the two men from the Free Flow garage. The man on the ground got up, his face scraped up from hitting the rough pavement. The two contemplated attacking Anderson, but when they saw Bolan, a look of recognition crossed their faces and they scurried back into the garage.

"Those bastards killed Darrick," Anderson said. "They killed my brother."

"Are you sure about that?" Bolan asked.

"There's no way in hell that Darrick's crash was an accident. There's no way that brake line came loose without someone disconnecting it. No way. Those sons of bitches killed my brother and I can prove it."

"How can you prove it?" Bolan asked. Anderson looked up at Bolan, suspicion in his eyes. "This is not a good place to talk," Bolan said. "Can I buy you a drink later?"

"I don't drink." After watching alcohol and drugs destroy Darrick's career, Eddie avoided the culture of hedonism that swirled around the racing circuit with an almost fanatical zeal, focusing on riding with the concentration of a Buddhist monk. The offer only increased his mistrust of the large stranger. "I've got to go. I've got a meeting." He rushed off before Bolan could question him further.

Bolan had no doubt that Eddie was lying about the meeting, but he couldn't fault the kid for not trusting him, especially if what he said about his brother was true. Bolan made a note to speak further with the young man, but for now the soldier did have a meeting, one he couldn't afford to miss.

THE ABRASIVE YOUNG American racer reminded Jameed Botros of his older brother, and as with the older Anderson, Botros felt it his duty to Allah to kill the man. People believed that Eddie Anderson differed from his brother, that he was not a slave to the vices that had destroyed Darrick's career, but Botros knew the younger man deceived those around him. He was first and foremost an American, and like all Americans he was weak. Botros had wanted to kill him the minute he laid eyes on him during the winter tire tests.

Now he might have a reason, but first he would have to clear it with bin Osman. Botros had gotten away with making a unilateral decision regarding the older Anderson brother; he dared not move against the younger brother without express permission from his superior. Botros had to present the Malaysian with a good reason why Eddie Anderson should be killed, and that is exactly what the impetuous youngster was giving him.

"You killed him!" the young rider shouted at Botros. Botros just smiled, knowing that when he reported Anderson's behavior to his supervisor, he would receive permission to eliminate the boy. "I know you killed him, and I can prove it!"

Anderson lunged toward Botros, but before he reached the Saudi, three sets of hands grabbed him and slammed him down on his back. Botros looked down at the face. The rage that twisted Anderson's features made him appear much older than his twenty-one years. "I am sure you are mistaken," Botros said. "It makes no sense that we would kill your brother."

"I don't give a shit if it makes sense or not! I know you did it!"

"Your brother's death was an accident. A tragic accident. His brakes failed."

"His brakes didn't fail. You loosened the brake lines and I can prove it!"

Botros had had enough of this foolish American. "Throw him out," he ordered his men in Arabic. For a small man, Anderson put up an impressive fight, but he was outnumbered four to one and after a drawn-out struggle, they ultimately ejected him from the garage complex. Before he was out the door Botros was in his office, calling bin Osman.

"We had an unexpected visitor this morning," Botros told his supervisor.

"Who might that be?" bin Osman asked.

"Eddie Anderson."

"Ah, the grieving brother."

"It would be more correct to call him the raging brother," Botros said. "He practically attacked me."

"Does he know?"

"He does. He even knows how we did it. He says he has proof, though how that is possible I don't know."

Bin Osman paused for a moment. "This young man could disrupt our plans."

"Do you want my men to take care of him?" Botros asked.

Again bin Osman paused. "No, we cannot draw unwanted attention to ourselves. He is too high-profile. Our plan must succeed. For that to happen, we have to be free to operate without the authorities investigating us, so we cannot engage in any activity that might attract such scrutiny. I know how we can deal with this."

"How?" Botros asked.

"You cannot give the authorities information you do not possess," bin Osman told Botros. "Just have faith that I will handle the problem. Unlike the way your men failed to handle our problem in Qatar last week."

Bin Osman hit a sore spot with the Saudi. The Malaysian had been enraged when the American gasoline peddler had escaped from the boat, but Botros had managed to calm him somewhat by reminding him that they still had the plutonium.

Getting the plutonium into the United States had been ridiculously easy. Team Free Flow had smuggled it into the country with all its other racing equipment. No customs inspector could ever hope to understand the esoteric collection of hardware and data-acquisitions electronic equipment used by a modern MotoGP racing team. It had been relatively simple to disguise the components needed to make a nuclear weapon among the racing equipment, even the Type B container used to transport the plutonium.

"When do you want us to move the material to the lab?" Botros asked, changing the subject.

"We'll be ready for it on Saturday, so plan to move it tomorrow night. But at the moment don't you have an appointment with the American?"

"Yes, he should be here soon. Do you want us to take care of him?"

"Like you took care of him last week? I think not. You and your men are to take no more risks, especially at the racetrack. I will take care of Mr. Cooper. Besides, I wish to meet a person who could dispatch five of your best men with such ease. Arrange for him to meet with me when I get to San Francisco tonight."

4

"I'm sorry I missed you last week Mr. Cooper," Botros told the Executioner after he sat down in the cramped office area set up in the back of the garage complex, "but it couldn't be avoided, as you know." Botros gave Bolan an artificially sweetened smile. "A terrible tragedy, and a blow to our organization," he said, referring to Darrick Anderson's death at Losail.

Bolan thought the man didn't seem terribly upset, especially given that the team's second rider, an aging Brazilian, was a perennial back marker who hadn't won a race in over a decade. Any chance of the team scoring points had died with Darrick Anderson, along with the attendant publicity his star power would have generated. Darrick's notoriety guaranteed television exposure whenever he was on a racetrack, even if he was only battling for eighth place. The only time the Brazilian racer ever appeared on a television screen was when he was getting lapped by the front runners.

In addition to his apparent indifference to the team's professional loss, Botros seemed not to have experienced a personal loss, either. In the close-knit fraternity of motorcycle racing, a racer getting killed devastated all the teams, especially the dead racer's team. It seemed as if the other teams grieved Darrick's loss more than Team Free Flow. Eddie's theory about his older brother's death could very well be true.

Bolan knew firsthand that Team Free Flow was affiliated with people who were more than capable of murder.

"I tried to contact you several times over the weekend to reschedule," Botros said, "but I couldn't reach you. I assumed you were indisposed."

"I was fishing," Bolan said. Botros' smile wavered momentarily at Bolan's reply, but returned more sickly sweet than ever.

"Well, Mr. Cooper, I hope you won't disappear on a fishing expedition this week. Musa bin Osman, Free Flow's vice president of racing, is flying in from Kuala Lumpur. He will be in San Francisco this evening and would very much like to meet with you. Our recent difficulties have been problematic for him. Free Flow's CEO is starting to question the expenses of racing, especially after the unfortunate incident last week. Getting sponsorship from your company would help smooth over the situation."

"You don't think this will create friction with Arexpo?" Bolan asked, referring to Team Free Flow's primary sponsor.

"Arexpo is an oil exploration company, not a refining company. They do not provide us with fuel. We purchase that," Botros said, referring to an Italian fuel company. "Of course we would have to analyze your fuel at the factory, then conduct extensive testing before we could come to an agreement. You really must discuss these details with my superior."

Bolan arranged to meet with bin Osman that night.

FOLLOWING THE MEETING, Bolan rode over to the Ducati garages in search of Eddie Anderson. Perhaps his supposed proof of his brother's murder might help him find the missing plutonium. It was a long shot, but right now it was the best shot Bolan had. No one at the Ducati garages had seen Eddie. The soldier overheard Daniel Asnorossa remark to his crew chief in Spanish, "Maybe he's off getting drunk, like his older brother."

Bolan walked around behind the garage area to where the riders' motor homes were parked. When practice got underway the following day, security in the area would tighten up, and by race day he knew he wouldn't get near the motor homes without an official escort, but this early in the week the area was practically deserted and security was lax. Only about half a dozen truly driven riders like Anderson and Asnorossa had shown up this early; everyone else would drift in later that night or early the next morning.

He found Anderson's motor home with the door wide open. The latch had been broken, and there were signs of some sort of struggle having taken place within the vehicle. Cushions had been knocked off the sofa and a broken cup and saucer lay on the floor in the kitchen area. A burner was still on under a stainless steel espresso pot on the stove and finely ground coffee was spread all over the counter and floor. Small drops of blood mixed with the coffee grounds and left a trail leading out the door. Bolan looked out the window above the stove and saw three men trying to stuff a struggling figure into the back of a Chevrolet Impala.

The Executioner exited the motor home and in several long strides he was almost to the car. The sight of the big man charging them momentarily distracted the kidnappers. Anderson took advantage of their paralysis, driving his knee into one of their crotches so hard he felt soft tissue rupturing in the man's groin. He may not have been a physically large man, but what mass he had consisted of strong bones wrapped in corded muscles, the result of constant training, years of wrestling the most powerful motorcycles on Earth around racetracks and good genetics. The wounded man collapsed to the ground, only to be replaced by two others, the driver and the front-seat passenger.

Bolan reached the melee at the moment the driver stepped out of the car and pointed an AK-47 his way. He had no time to draw his own weapon but from the angle at which the man held the rifle against his hip the soldier could see that the shooter's aim was high. The Executioner dived into the grass beneath the stream of bullets, sliding into the shooter's legs and knocking him back into the car. Bolan leapt to his feet, grabbing the hot rifle barrel on his way up and wrenching it away from the shooter's hands.

Meanwhile, Eddie Anderson fought like a demonic howler monkey against the two would-be kidnappers, but they were proving too much for him. Bolan raised the gun barrel over his head and brought the wooden stock down square in the shooter's face. When he pulled the stock from the man's face, which no longer bore any resemblance to a human face, he spun around and slammed the gore-covered rifle butt into the temple of one of the men attacking Anderson. The man fell to the ground.

Anderson had the other attacker on the ground, his knees pinning the man's arms and his fist pumping into the man's face. Anderson looked as if he might beat the man to death, but the fellow whose scrotum he had ruptured rose up and pulled him off the man before he could deliver the killing blow. The man Anderson had been beating struggled to his feet, blood spraying from a deep gash near his left cheekbone. He reached behind his back. Bolan knew he was going for a weapon so he swung the rifle stock around again and caught him right across his right temple, hitting him so hard that a geyser of blood erupted from the left side of his head. His eyes rolled back and he fell to the ground.

Bolan flipped the rifle around as he spun to see the remaining kidnapper holding Anderson in front of him, a 9 mm Glock 17 pressed to Anderson's right temple. Bolan put the hooded post of the front sight on the portion of the kidnapper's head that was the farthest away from Anderson. Though he had no idea how well sighted in the AK was, at this short range the executioner could see the gun barrel was pointed past Anderson's head. He gave the trigger a short squeeze, firing off just one round even though the selector was on full auto.

That round did the business. The man flew back and dropped, his torso falling against the back seat through the open door. Anderson whirled around, ready to fight some more, but there was no one left to fight. The four would-be kidnappers all lay dead at their feet.

The dead man looked Asian, possibly Filipino, judging by what was left of their faces. Laguna Seca was still relatively empty and so far no one had arrived on the scene, but Bolan could tell the gunshots had attracted attention because of the sirens he heard coming their way. He looked inside the car and pulled out a magazine. Bolan knew it would be filled with blow-in subscription cards, so he shook it until four cards fell out. He dipped each of the kidnapper's right-hand index fingers in blood and made fingerprint imprints on the card stock. He had the cards in the vest pocket of his sport jacket before the police arrived.

Four squad cars skidded to a stop on the grass. "You're no gas salesman, are you?" Anderson asked the soldier.

"I'm a sales representative for the manufacturer of quality

racing fuels," Bolan said, "but I had some combat training when I was in the military."

"Whatever," Anderson said. "I don't care. I'm just glad you came along when you did. Thank you."

BOTH ANDERSON AND BOLAN spent the next several hours at the Monterey Police Department describing what had happened. Since Bolan wasn't suspected of anything besides being a good Samaritan who stopped the kidnapping of a celebrity, they allowed him to ride his motorcycle to the precinct. This enabled him to stash his weapons before he went through the metal detector at the security checkpoint in the precinct's entrance. Bolan's credentials as Matt Cooper were impeccable, and even though his brutal slaying of the attackers raised suspicions, his reactions were justifiable, and they'd had a beneficial result for the department. Having one of the world's top motorcycle racers kidnapped under their noses would have been a tremendous embarrassment to the force. Bolan was allowed to leave before Anderson, who remained behind because he wanted to tell the police his theories about his brother's murder. After the attempted kidnapping, the authorities were much more interested in what had happened to Darrick Anderson. So was the Executioner, but at the moment he had other matters to attend to.

As soon as he was back at his hotel, Bolan scanned the fingerprints he'd pulled from the corpses on his portable scanner and sent them to Stony Man Farm. He wanted to find out who he'd just killed.

Within half an hour Aaron Kurtzman was on the phone with that information. "You were right about their being Filipinos, Striker," Kurtzman said. "These were some particularly badass Filipinos, too, known members of Jemaah Islamiah."

"So what's the connection between these guys and Team Free Flow?"

Kurtzman paused, obviously reading through the information he'd uncovered in the short time since Bolan had sent him the fingerprints. "It all seems to point back to Musa bin Osman."

"Speak of the devil," Bolan said. "I have an appointment with him in three hours."

"There's something else you should know," Kurtzman said. "The men you killed also had strong ties to the BNG."

Bolan knew the BNG—the Bahala Na Gang—was one of the most powerful Filipino street gangs. Originally formed by inmates in the notorious jails of the Philippines in the early 1940s, the BNG eventually spread its operations around the globe. Originally *Bahala Na* meant "God willing," in Tagalog, but in recent generations the term had come to mean a more fatalistic "whatever." Fatalism defined the BNG, and fatality followed it from the Philippines to North America, where the organization had evolved into an especially violent criminal syndicate. The BNG was strong in the San Francisco area.

"I didn't have time to examine the bodies before the police arrived," Bolan said. "I didn't see any question marks." Each member of the BNG tattooed a question mark symbol somewhere on his body. "So these guys are hooked up with al Qaeda now?"

"At least the four men you killed today were," Kurtzman said. "It might be more accurate to say that Jemaah Islamiah is hooked up with the BNG. My guess is that they're just hiring the BNG for muscle."

"That would be my guess, too," the Executioner said.

"But they're good muscle," Kurtzman replied. "Watch your back tonight, Striker."

"How'd they get into the paddock?"

Kurtzman took a moment to answer, meaning he was once again looking through the reports he and his team had generated. "Says here that they were posing as reporters for *City Rider,* a San Francisco-based motorcycle magazine."

"Has our little altercation at the track this morning attracted any attention?"

"Attention? It's being broadcast on every major news channel nonstop. You couldn't have attracted more attention. All the major newshounds are already on the scene. I don't know what's going to be harder for you—finding the plutonium or dodging those nitwits."

"I'm not worried. They'll be gone tomorrow, chasing after some little girl who's fallen down a well or something," Bolan speculated.

"You're probably right about that," Kurtzman said.

"What have the police found so far?" Bolan asked.

"I've hacked into their computer system, and it doesn't look like much. They haven't connected the BNG to al Qaeda yet, and they probably won't; they've already written the attack off as an attempted kidnapping by the BNG."

"That makes sense," Bolan said. "Kidnapping is the BNG's primary source of income in the Philippines. And it makes sense that they'd go after Anderson."

Bolan knew that while motorcycle racing was a relatively obscure activity in the United States, it was extremely popular in the rest of the world and the top MotoGP riders were superstars. These young gladiators ranked among the most popular athletes on the planet, and a star rider such as Eddie Anderson or Daniel Asnorossa could earn ten million dollars a year or more. All of that made Anderson an obvious kidnapping target for a criminal organization like the BNG.

"Have they called in the Feds?" Bolan asked.

"I don't think they asked for federal assistance, but the FBI has already involved itself." Kurtzman said.

"That's just one more thing I have to worry about," Bolan said. "I'd say there's a fifty-fifty chance that the Feds will uncover the al Qaeda connection. If they do, they're just going to get in the way of finding the plutonium. Any chance you could misdirect them, Bear?"

"Striker, you know that would be wrong."

"Meaning you can do it?"

"Piece of cake."

"Good. Could you get Barb on the line?"

Kurtzman passed the phone to Stony Man's mission controller.

"What do you need, Striker?" Price asked.

"I need some security on the Anderson kid. Do you have any blacksuits you can put on it?" Blacksuits were operatives, often law-enforcement officials, who had been through advanced training at Stony Man Farm, though they never knew exactly where they had received the training. This training helped them better perform their jobs, and in return they often assisted Stony Man operatives in the field.

"I'm one step ahead of you," Price said. "I've already sent one of our best men in the area, a former detective with the San Francisco PD named Delbert Osborne, to guard Anderson."

"Thanks, Barb. That's one less thing I have to worry about."

The maître d' at Masa's Restaurant, a nice eating establishment on San Francisco's Nob Hill, led Bolan down to the Wine Cellar, the restaurant's private meeting room. Musa bin Osman had wanted to meet in his suite at a nearby hotel, but Bolan had insisted on taking his potential business partner out to dinner. Most likely bin Osman knew that the soldier was just trying to evade whatever trap he might have planned by meeting in a public place, but the Malaysian business man couldn't protest too vehemently without giving away his intentions.

Bin Osman arrived with an entourage of four men who seemed uncomfortable in their bespoke suits. These hard-looking men seemed like they'd be more at home in prison jump suits. They were definitely not cut from the same corporate cloth as bin Osman, and they said little while Bolan and bin Osman went through the motions and discussed the details of CCP Petroleum possibly sponsoring Team Free Flow Racing. The Executioner had studied the intricacies of sponsoring a MotoGP race team on the flight from Qatar, and he proved remarkably adept at portraying a racing fuel sales rep.

Not that he expected bin Osman to buy a word of it. Bolan was certain that the Malaysian knew every detail about what had transpired in Qatar. The real reason he and bin Osman attended the meeting was because they wanted to size each other up.

"I'm glad you could make it to dinner tonight, Mr. Cooper," bin Osman said, "given the adventure you had at the track today. The television portrayed you as some sort of superhero."

"I got lucky," Bolan replied. "I remembered my military training."

"Were you with Special Forces?"

"Just a run-of-the-mill grunt," Bolan said. "I did have some sniper training, but otherwise nothing out of the ordinary."

"Ah, a sniper," bin Osman said. "Retired, I hope."

"Correct, and more than a bit rusty, but when I saw the attempted kidnapping, I was still able to do what I needed to do."

"You seem more than capable," the Malaysian said.

Bin Osman continued to grill Bolan throughout dinner. By the time he'd finished his dessert, the Executioner had no doubt that bin Osman intended to kill him. And maybe he would, but not before Bolan retrieved the plutonium. And if this turned out to be the Executioner's last mission, he intended to take bin Osman with him into the next world. When he looked at the man sitting across from him at the table, he saw something he'd seen far too many times in his life—pure evil.

MUSA BIN OSMAN needed to size up the American before having him dispatched. He'd learned that Cooper was not affiliated with CCP Oil, though he would not have learned that going through proper channels. Whoever had created Cooper's identity had been good, and every attempt by bin Osman to discredit the Cooper's credentials had proved fruitless.

Cooper certainly looked the part. He dressed well enough so that he would fit in at a restaurant like Masa's, but not so well that anyone would wonder why he worked for a living. His clothes were expensive, but off-the-rack and not bespoke, though his broad shoulders obviously required some tailoring. Everything was perfect, from his sport jacket—which likely disguised at least one firearm, and perhaps two, judging by the nearly undetectable square-edged bulges beneath his armpits and at his waistline—to his shoes. Cooper didn't just dress like a sales representative; he dressed like a very successful sales representative.

Bin Osman hadn't been able to learn anything about Cooper through proper channels, but he'd had better luck going through unofficial channels. CCP Oil had many ties with the Islamic world, including groups that bin Osman counted among his own acquaintances. Through his connections with such groups in Asia and the Middle East, he'd learned that no one within the CCP organization seemed to personally know this Cooper. This wasn't unheard of when it came to an outside sales representative, but bin Osman already knew that Cooper was no peddler of racing fuel.

Who he really was presented another question entirely. It was as if Matt Cooper had emerged from some chrysalis as a fully formed warrior. He seemingly had no past. This was, of course, impossible, and throughout the evening bin Osman studied the American as if through a microscope. Only one thing was certain; Cooper was dangerous.

Whatever his name, the man seated across the table from him wasn't sizing him up. Cooper knew for certain what he was dealing with when it came to his adversary; of this bin Osman had no doubt. He knew that this secretive warrior would have no trouble killing him. Rather the big man sized up the situation. Bin Osman admired the man's certitude and his efficiency. He would welcome the chance to practice the art of torture on such a specimen, but he realized that this man was not to be taken lightly. Although bin Osman ached to know how much the man would take before he snapped, he had a mission and this man posed a serious threat to the completion of that mission. No, he would have to deny himself that pleasure and dispatch of this man as efficiently as possible.

After Cooper left the table, bin Osman produced a cell phone from the vest pocket of his linen suit. "He's left the building," he said into the phone. "Get ready."

BOLAN DIDN'T HAVE TO WAIT LONG before bin Osman made his move. While he stood beside his motorcycle parked outside the restaurant and put on his riding gear, a black Hummer H2 with dark tinted windows rolled by at too slow a pace for the occupants not to be checking him out. With one eye on the slow-moving SUV, the soldier folded his sport jacket and put it in the top box over the bike's rear fender. Then he put on his two-piece riding suit, prepared to draw his weapon and take cover should the Hummer occupants start shooting at him. After the SUV rolled around the corner, Bolan changed from his dress shoes into his riding boots, then put on his helmet and riding gloves. He took his time, watching to see if the Hummer reappeared. Sure enough, minutes later the Hummer rolled by again.

Bolan waited until it once again rounded the corner, then rode away from the curb. He made a left turn onto Stockton Street and watched his mirrors until he saw the Hummer turn onto the street about three cars behind him. The Executioner made a left turn onto Pine Street without signaling his turn. Traffic was relatively light on the big four-lane street and when the Hummer came around the corner there were no cars between the soldier and the big, black SUV.

The Hummer accelerated hard, but Bolan jammed on the throttle, hoisting the front wheel of the motorcycle as if gravity had no effect on the big bike. He was doing seventy miles per hour by the time he reached Powell Street. The soldier checked his mirror and saw that the black H2 was driving even faster than he was. Bolan cranked the throttle to the stop, riding like a crazed kid with a death wish—motorcyclists called them "squids" because of the squid-like stains they left on the pavement when they crashed—and was doing ninety by the time he reached Taylor Street. He saw that the light in the intersection had turned from yellow to red. He knew he'd get through before the Taylor Street signal lights turned green, so kept the throttle pinned, sending the speedometer past one hundred.

By the time the Hummer reached the intersection, the signal light on Taylor Street had been green long enough that cars were entering the intersection. The Hummer ran the red light and nailed the front bumper of an older Chrysler minivan. The bumper flew off as if it had been shot out of a cannon and the minivan spun off the road, landing on the sidewalk.

When Bolan got to the intersection of Pine and Hyde, he tapped the rear brake, put his foot down and pinned the throttle again, breaking the rear tire loose and sliding out, executing a perfect Super-motard-style right-hand turn, hanging the rear wheel out all the way onto Hyde Street. This left him going the wrong way on a one-way street, so he aimed his bike between two cars waiting at the traffic light and passed between their two lanes, the hand guards on his bike knocking the sideview mirrors off of the cars on his left and right, missing their doors by millimeters. The Hummer screamed around the corners and didn't miss the doors, or any other parts of the cars.

Bolan looked in his mirrors and saw the two cars spinning up onto the sidewalks on either side of the road. This slowed the Hummer somewhat, but Bolan still hadn't shaken it off his tail.

When Bolan crested California Street he caught nearly a foot of air and landed on the back tire. He kept the throttle pinned as he roared up Hyde Street, which went back to being a two-way street after it intersected with California. Bolan rode at triple-digit speeds down Hyde Street, keeping just ahead of his pursuers. He rode over the Broadway Tunnel and saw a car coming at him on Broadway Street. If he kept his speed up, he might make it through before the car entered the intersection so he kept the throttle twisted. He ran the Stop sign and squeezed through ahead of the car, but again the Hummer wasn't so lucky. It sheared the car in two; the passenger compartment skidded through the intersection while the front clip disintegrated beneath the Hummer's mangled bumper.

The Hummer looked like a wreck. Its headlights were gone, its fenders crumpled and torn, but judging by the lack of steam, the radiator was intact, probably thanks to the gigantic brush guard on the front of the truck. It had driving lights on the roof that lit up the night much brighter than any headlights. Bolan rode as fast as he dared without hurting any innocent bystanders, but if he kept this up, the Hummer bearing down on him was either going to kill him or kill someone else. The soldier had to bring this to an end. With Lombard Street, San Francisco's famous narrow road that switchbacked down toward the sea, coming up on his right, he formulated a plan to do just that.

When he neared Lombard Street, he slowed a bit to let the Hummer close in on him. With its prey in its sights, the Hummer sped up to run down the Executioner, but just as it neared him, Bolan swerved to the right and jammed on the brakes. On most bikes it would have been the start of a terrible crash, but because of BMW's anti-lock brakes Bolan was able to stop almost instantly while the Hummer sailed past him. Physics were on the soldier's side; six hundred pounds of motorcycle stopped much more quickly than six thousand pounds of sport utility vehicle. and Bolan was able to hang a hard right onto Lombard Street and fly down to the intersection with Leavenworth Street as the big Hummer screeched to a stop halfway down the block. Bolan threw the big motorcycle from right to left to right like an overgrown BMX bicycle and was past the turn onto the Montclair Terrace, a dead-end street that T-boned Lombard Street about halfway through the switchback section between Hyde and Leavenworth, by the time the Hummer started descending the wildly twisting street. Bolan could hear the Hummer crashing into parked cars and banging off the short concrete retainer walls that ran alongside the street as he rode to the bottom of the hill.

At Leavenworth Street, Bolan hung a hard right and rode up on the sidewalk. He parked the bike and ran to the edge of a garage on the street corner, drawing his Desert Eagle on the way. He leaned up against the edge of the garage, waiting for the Hummer to crash its way down. As the cab of the Hummer appeared in his field of vision, the Executioner lined up the sights of the gun right about where he figured the driver would be sitting, compensating for the change in angle that the spalling of the glass would cause. He emptied a magazine into the glass. His calculations must have been fairly accurate because the Hummer ran through the intersection and crashed into the corner of the building on the northeast corner of the intersection.

Bolan ran toward the wreck, reloading on the way. He

hoped to find a survivor, but before he reached the vehicle a man stepped out of the rear door, which had flown open on impact with the building, and raised a SAR-21 rifle, a bull-pup-style rifle built in Singapore—and never legally imported into the U.S. market. He fired. The man could barely stand, and his shaky stance made his shooting inaccurate. The 5.56 mm NATO bullets from the stubby gun went wide. Bolan raised the Desert Eagle and drilled a 240-grain hollow point through the shooter's forehead. Bolan kept the gun trained on the open door in case anyone else inside the vehicle might try to attack him.

When he got to the truck, he could see no one was going to cause him any problems. No one in the cab had worn a seat belt, so the air bags that deployed in the front seat hadn't been much help to its occupants. Judging from the .44 caliber hole in the driver's temple, he hadn't been alive when the air bags deployed. The front-seat passenger must have been holding a SAR-21 between his legs because the combined force of the crash and the airbag deployment had driven the stubby barrel into his throat, burying it all the way up to the plastic foregrip. It had hit the jugular and the man had bled out before Bolan reached the Hummer.

The last man in the cab was still alive, but just barely. Like the others, he was a Filipino, and Bolan saw the telltale question mark tattoo on the bare shoulder that showed beneath his dirty wife beater undershirt. He was conscious, but blood ran from his mouth, nose and ears, and he looked like he was fading out. Bolan grabbed his shirt and gently slapped his face, trying to get him to wake up. The man's eyes opened and he smiled. Then he spit blood and tooth fragments at the soldier and laughed.

"Who are you working for?" Bolan asked.

"Fuck you, man," the man—he was really just a kid—said, then laughed again.

"You working for Botros?" The kid said nothing, but a look of recognition crossed his face when Bolan said the name. "Do you know where they've taken the plutonium?"

"What are you talking about plutonium?" the kid said. "You white boys need to lay off that meth."

"Didn't you know?" Bolan asked. "Your boss has brought enough plutonium into the country to build a bomb so big it could blow up this city and take Oakland with it. He's not even going to have to pay you what he owes you because he's going to kill you. He's going to kill your homies, your mother, your sister, your baby momma, and everyone you've ever known. You fools are helping to get your own families killed."

"Man, you keep talking that shit, I'm gonna cut you." The kid kept talking tough, but Bolan could see real fear in his eyes. He'd seen or heard something that convinced him there was truth to what the Executioner said.

"Go ahead and try," Bolan said. "But I'm not the person who's going to kill your entire family. How does it feel to help someone kill everyone you've ever known?"

The man spit again, but this time he didn't spit at Bolan. Instead he just cleared his mouth and tried to speak. "I saw it," he said. "In the warehouse. We unloaded the cask."

"You saw what?" the Executioner asked. "Where?"

"The cask. We helped unload a heavy steel cask."

The kid choked and coughed up a lot of blood. Bolan knew he wasn't going to last long.

"Where? Where is the cask?"

"Santa Cruz." The kid coughed up more blood, but this time he couldn't clear his throat. "Near the railroad tracks."

He coughed a couple of times, desperately trying to catch his breath, and finally dropped his head, silent. Bolan checked his pulse and found none. He could hear sirens fast approaching. He ran back to his motorcycle and roared down Leavenworth Street towards the freeway.

"BEAR, I NEED YOU TO ACCESS a spy satellite for me," Bolan said to Aaron Kurtzman. "Something going over Santa Cruz." The soldier had contacted the Stony Man Farm computer expert the moment he'd returned to his hotel room in Monterey after his trip to San Francisco.

"I can get photography at twenty-three-minute intervals," Kurtzman replied. "Unless whoever you're looking for knew the exact orbits of our satellites and had perfect timing, I should be able to find something. What am I looking for?"

"Some guys unloading a heavy cask or container from a van or truck at a warehouse."

"Are we looking for a Type B container filled with ten kilos of plutonium 239?"

"Something along those lines," the soldier replied.

"I need something more," Kurtzman said. "There aren't a lot of warehouses in Santa Cruz, but what you just gave me could describe almost every delivery to every single one of them.

"Look near the railroad tracks." The soldier had taken a detour through Santa Cruz on his way back from San Francisco and he'd identified several likely warehouse facilities that were along the railroad tracks that ran through town just south of the Cabrillo Highway—California's famous Highway One, also known as the Coast Highway. He gave Kurtzman the GPS coordinates of the prime candidates.

"Anything else that could help me?"

"This might be a long shot, but look for a black Hummer H2 with dark tinted windows."

"That's not much."

"Do your best, Bear."

The sun poked up over the hills to the east when the Executioner finally laid down for some sleep. Less than two hours later, a sharp rap at the door woke him up. He threw on the large robe the hotel had provided, sliding a Fairbairn-Sykes Fighting Knife into the sleeve in case he needed it. Then he grabbed a wire hanger from the closet, untwisted it and used it to hold a black shirt in front of the peephole as he stood to the side of the door. When no shots came through the door, he chanced a look through the peephole.

"Oh hell," Bolan said to himself when he saw the two conservatively dressed Americans at the door. Their dark suits, unstylish neck ties and humorless demeanor meant one of only two possibilities, and since they were too old to be Mormon missionaries they had to be the FBI agents Kurtzman had warned him about earlier.

Bolan opened the door. "Can I help you?" he asked.

"Federal Bureau of Investigation," the taller of the two men said. "I'm Agent Smith and this is Agent Kowalski." They both showed Bolan their badges. Bolan inspected the badges so he could be reasonably certain they were legit before letting the two men into his room. "We'd like to discuss yesterday's events," Smith said.

"Did I leave something out of my report to the police yesterday?" the Executioner asked? "I believe I was thorough."

"We've read the report," Kowalski, the shorter of the two said. "You were very thorough."

"Is there a problem?" Bolan asked.

"No problem," Kowalski said. "We just have some questions to help us tie up a few loose ends. Why were you looking for Eddie Anderson when he was kidnapped?"

"I'd had a conversation with him prior to attending a meeting earlier in the morning."

"A conversation about what?" Smith asked.

"About his late brother," Bolan said. "The young man seemed upset."

"Why did you care that he was upset?" Kowalski asked. "You have no chance of sponsoring a major team like the Ducati factory squad. What does Anderson mean to you?"

"He is a great racer, and I'm a fan. And he seemed to be in a great deal of pain over the loss of his brother. As I said, he seemed upset. I didn't have another meeting until the evening and Mr. Anderson had no practice sessions until today, so I thought I'd pay him a visit."

"Lucky for him that you did," Smith commented, prompting Kowalski to glare at his taller partner.

"Our files say that you work for CCP Petroleum," Kowalski said.

"Correct," Bolan replied. "Is that a crime?"

"No," Kowalski replied, "but killing four men might be."

"I don't understand," Bolan said. "Those men clearly meant to kidnap or kill Eddie Anderson, and they tried to kill me. That doesn't justify the use of lethal force?"

"It certainly does," Smith said. "I don't think anyone here is implying that you have committed a crime of any kind. As my partner said, we're just trying to tie up a few loose ends."

"So you said. Gentlemen, I've given all the information I have to the authorities. I've had a very difficult day and I still have work to do. I'll be glad to answer any questions, but please, let's not go around and around. Please get to your point."

"We have no point, Mr. Cooper," Kowalski said. "We just need to tie up a few loose ends."

6

After wasting nearly two hours with the FBI agents, Bolan made his way to the track where he found Eddie Anderson in the middle of Friday morning practice. This was the young American's home race, and he'd already won countless races on this track when he was racing Superbikes in the U.S. His lap times reflected his familiarity with the track and before the first session was over, not only had he set the fastest times, he'd unofficially broken the track record. Tomorrow he would almost certainly break the official record for a qualifying lap and he would likely set a race lap record during Sunday's main event. If he lived that long.

While the youngster circled the track, Bolan watched for Osborne, the blacksuit who was supposed to be watching Anderson. Either the man was very good or he was absent because the soldier found no sign of him. He hoped Osborne was that good but he doubted it. If the man had been present, Bolan would have found some trace of him. It was not a good sign.

When Anderson finished his session, Bolan met him as he walked back to his motor home. "Hey," the young man said by way of greeting.

"Hey," the Executioner responded in kind.

The young rider looked the soldier up and down. "I still

can't figure out what your story is," he said. "You sure ain't no fuel salesman."

"You want to see my credentials, perhaps speak with my director?"

"Whatever," Anderson said. "At least you ain't no pervert, near as I can tell, anyway."

"I do my best," Bolan responded.

"So what is your story? What I saw you do yesterday, I've never seen anyone do something like that before."

"I've had a little martial arts training," Bolan said.

Anderson seemed to buy that. "I take it that yesterday wasn't the first time you killed a man with your bare hands."

Bolan didn't respond.

"I'm just glad you're here Mr. Cooper."

"Please, it's Matt. Haven't you hired someone for protection? It might be wise, given what happened yesterday."

"Some cop from the San Francisco Police Department showed up yesterday evening, said he was supposed to keep an eye on me."

"Where is he?" Bolan asked.

"I canned him," Anderson said. "I told him I didn't need a babysitter, and told him to get the hell out of here."

"And he left?"

"Hell no! I had to call security and have him escorted out of here."

"You don't worry about another attempt on your life?" Bolan asked.

"They had their chance. They won't try anything again, at least not here." The young man sounded sure of himself. Bolan felt less confident about the kid's safety.

"You said you have proof that your brother was killed," Bolan said. "What proof?"

"I'll show you." Bolan followed Anderson into his motor home, where Anderson dug out a banjo-bolt fitting wrapped in a grease rag and handed it to the Executioner.

"What's this?" Bolan asked.

"It's the brake line connection from Darrick's bike," Anderson said.

"How'd you get it?"

"I stole it from the Free Flow garage complex at Losail. They won't miss it; they're supposed to examine the wreckage but they have no interest in it. They don't seem to give much of a shit about what happened to Darrick."

"I got that impression myself," Bolan said. "Why is this important?"

"Look at the thread on the male fitting." Bolan did. The thread seemed like new, except for the first two rungs, which were stripped clean.

"That bolt was never tightened down. Someone deliberately just barely got the threads started, tightening them just enough so that they'd hold as long as there was no pressure applied to the brakes. As soon as someone grabbed a handful of brake, that thing popped right off," Anderson said.

It looked to Bolan like the kid was on to something. "Why would anyone want to kill your brother?" he asked.

"Time was, just about everyone wanted to kill him, back when he was banging cocaine and drinking twenty-four hours a day. Even before that. When he had the championship, he was an ass—arrogant, cocky, rude, abusive. Killing him even crossed my mind once or twice, especially after our parents were killed in a car accident and he didn't even bother to come to the funeral. Said he had a tire test in Jerez, Spain, but he didn't show up for that either," Anderson said angrily. He paused.

"But he'd changed. He wasn't the same person he was back then. He was doing great. It was like I had my brother back." Anderson pointed to the bolts from his brother's bike. "And then those bastards took him away from me."

"It doesn't make sense. Why'd they kill their top rider?" the Executioner asked.

"I don't know," Anderson said. "I do know that they don't care one whit about motorcycle racing. I don't know why they're even here."

Bolan suspected that the reason they were here was because they intended to commit a major act of terrorism somewhere on the west coast, but there was know point in mentioning that to the younger Anderson brother. And the soldier suspected that the reason they killed Darrick was because he either knew something or they were afraid he might know something. One thing was certain—they were dealing with some dangerous men.

"I suppose you think I'm crazy, just like everyone else," Anderson said.

"No, I believe you. I know these men are capable of committing murder," Bolan said.

Eddie Anderson looked at the soldier. "That's strange information for a fuel salesman to have."

"My company does its research on potential business partners," Bolan said. "These are some bad men, and they're capable of anything. They're capable of killing your brother, and they're capable of killing you. I wish you'd reconsider letting the police officer protect you."

"Hell no! I can take care of myself. I always have and I always will."

Bolan respected the kid's dedication to self-sufficiency, but he knew that this inexperienced youth was no match for a group of trained and dedicated terrorists.

"If you're so good at taking care of yourself," the Executioner said, "how come every time I see you someone is either throwing you out of a building or throwing you into a car?"

Bolan could tell he'd hit a nerve.

The kid's eyes narrowed. "I think it's time for you to leave. I have to prepare for afternoon practice," Anderson said.

EDDIE ANDERSON missed his apex on Laguna Seca's turn two, the famous Andretti Hairpin. He couldn't get his head into the moment, a moment that saw his negotiating one of the world's most challenging racetracks aboard what was perhaps the fastest motorcycle on Earth. He couldn't shake his brother's death out of his head.

He made the next several corners as if on autopilot, and as the next right-hand corner approached, he couldn't remember if it was Turn Five or Turn Six. It turned out to be the more rounded Turn Five and not the sharper-edged Turn Six, though he once again missed his apex because he'd mentally prepared for Turn Six. These were stupid, rookie mistakes and Anderson chastised himself for making them.

He cleared his mind by Turn Six and executed the corner perfectly, getting a hard drive up the hill toward the corkscrew. He threw his bike to the left, down the hill into the corkscrew, then made a beautiful arcing turn to the right, apexing perfectly at the bottom of the hill as he left the corkscrew, hitting one hundred and fifty miles per hour before braking for Turn Nine. Anderson's technique for negotiating the corkscrew was nearly perfect, almost as good as his brother's had once been. Darrick had been universally regarded as the king of Laguna Seca.

Thinking of Darrick once again distracted the younger Anderson brother and he braked too late for Turn Nine—Rainey Curve—and he ran wide, toward the gravel trap at the edge of the track. It was what racers called "the kitty litter." He'd just about saved himself from an embarrassing crash when his teammate Danny Asnorossa came by off the main racing line. Asnorossa crossed in front of Anderson and clipped the American's front tire with his rear tire, slamming Anderson's bike down in a low slide.

Both Anderson and the bike slid off the track, the bike sliding on its side, and Anderson flipping through the air. He saw a rapid series of images—earth-sky-earth-sky-earth-sky—before he finally came to a stop in the gravel. Before getting up, he took stock of his body. Nothing appeared to be damaged except his pride. He walked over to the bike and picked it up. He'd lost a footpeg and his brake lever was broken off, but the motorcycle was still running. With the help of the corner workers who had already descended on the scene, he got it out of the "kitty litter" and rode it back to the pits. It appeared to be just cosmetic damage that his crew could repair so he wouldn't have to get out his backup bike.

He would have to get his mind right before the race on Sunday or he wasn't going to win. If he kept riding like he had been during that afternoon's practice, he wouldn't even survive Sunday's race.

7

"Striker, I think I know where they're keeping the plutonium," Kurtzman said over the secure line connected to Bolan's cell phone. "Better yet, I'm sure I know what they plan to do with it."

"What's that?" Bolan asked.

"You've probably figured out how popular racing is in the rest of the world."

"I've noticed."

"It's getting more popular here, too. When the big races come to town, they bring out a galaxy of stars, politicians, and international dignitaries who attend the event. This year the attendees will include the newly elected president of Egypt—he's a young pro-Western reformer—along with the king of Jordan, another Islamic moderate, and the youngest son of the crown prince of the House of Saud, who is widely believed to be running Saudi Arabia. He's popular with his people and has good relations with our government. These three men represent our best hopes for stability in the Middle East. And all three are big racing fans."

"In other words," Bolan said, "just about every pro-Western leader in the Islamic world will be in the same place at the same time."

"You got it. I did some poking around and all three are

staying in hotels on Nob Hill. All three are flying in Sunday morning and all three plan to stay over Sunday night and leave on Monday."

"Someone could take out all three by setting off a Hiroshima-sized bomb, which is what we're talking about here, right, Bear?"

"You are correct, sir."

"If they set off a bomb like that at the race, they would strike a fatal blow to moderate Islamic regimes in the Middle East and probably unleash a fundamentalist firestorm across the region. Plus they'd take out a symbol of Western decadence in the process."

"Correct again," Kurtzman said.

Bolan contemplated the situation. "Sometimes it would be better to be wrong," he told Kurtzman. "How about the warehouse?"

"There really is only one that fits the parameters you gave me yesterday. It's located on Fair Avenue, right next to the tracks. A white delivery van dropped off a load there late Monday morning, a heavy load, judging from the before and after photos of the van. The springs were compressed so far that the van's bumper was practically dragging on the pavement on the way to the warehouse. It looked like a dog dragging its butt across carpet. On the way back, the van rode a full six inches higher in the back."

"Can you estimate the weight of the load?"

"I had three-inch resolution from my spy satellite so I got the license plate. It was a rental with a one-ton chassis. The van was easily loaded fifty percent over capacity, so I'd say we're looking at something weighing three thousand pounds or more."

"Like a small Type B container?"

"Affirmative," Kurtzman said. "There was even a black

Hummer H2 with dark tinted windows parked out front while the van was inside the warehouse unloading the cargo."

"Who rented the van?

"A construction company, which turned out to be fictitious, as did the person who signed all the paperwork.

"So we got nothing on the rental?" the soldier asked.

"Not quite nothing," Kurtzman replied. "The surveillance cameras showed four Filipinos picking up the van. One of them had a question mark tattooed on his forearm."

"Anything more?" Bolan asked.

"The warehouse has been under heavy guard twenty-four hours a day since Monday."

"Rent-a-cops?"

"Nope. Gang bangers, by the look of them. I can't quite be sure, but it looks like one of them has a question mark tattooed on his shoulder. They also appear to be armed, judging by the bulges above their waistbands. They've been taking eight-hour shifts, and there appears to be at least four on guard at any one time. There are probably more inside. Someone has something of value in that facility."

"I'll check it out right away, but first I need one last favor from you."

"You name it, Striker."

"Can you figure out a way to keep those two Feds out of my face? I've experienced physical torture that was more pleasant than spending a few minutes with those two."

"Consider it done."

Santa Cruz, California

BOLAN'S DECISION to rent a motorcycle proved a good one. He was one of tens of thousands of motorcyclists riding the coastal highway between Santa Cruz and San Francisco during the weekend of the big race, though Bolan was probably the only rider with an FN P90 submachine gun slung beneath his riding jacket.

He'd had Kissinger fit the rifle with a Leupold Mark 4 CQ/T rifle scope, allowing the soldier to accurately fire the bullpup subgun at ranges past two hundred yards, which was farther than he was likely shoot in an urban environment. The scope had an advanced light-gathering coating on the glass, letting the soldier see his targets in extremely low light conditions, as well as a reticle that could be lit or unlit for use in various lighting conditions. Kissinger knew all of the Executioner's measurements and could set the eye relief on almost any gun so that it was near spot-on perfect when it reached the soldier in the field, and he always zeroed the optics at one hundred yards except on high-powered rifles, as per Bolan's preference. The soldier seldom took shots at much longer ranges than that, and if he needed to do so, he knew how to compensate for any caliber of rifle that he might be called upon to use.

The little rifle held fifty rounds of ammunition, and Bolan had four loaded magazines in his jacket, two in the front vest pocket designed to hold a water bladder and one in each inside vest pocket. The unusual design of the rifle placed the clear plastic box magazine on top of the barrel, under the optical platform. Since the gun was of the bullpup design, the receiver was in the rear of the gun, at the back of the buttstock, so it wasn't much longer than his Beretta 93-R when the sound-suppressor was attached.

Once again he wore the experimental lightweight armored vest that Kissinger had developed under his riding suit. Underneath that he wore his skintight blacksuit. The vest would stop the 5.56 mm rounds fired by the SAR-21 rifles from Singapore and most other common rifle calibers he'd likely run across, but it wouldn't stop the rounds in his P90. The steel-cored rounds would penetrate forty-eight layers of Kevlar when fired from a weapon like the P90. He didn't know if the gang bangers guarding the warehouse would be wearing body armor, but if they were, the soldier was prepared.

Bolan rode to Santa Cruz on Highway One, noting that there were people milling around the warehouse when he rode past Fair Avenue. Traffic was heavy and he moved slowly, allowing him to get a good look at the building. The sun was just starting to set; in another hour it would be dark enough to make his move. The soldier rode up the Coast Highway until he got to Laguna Road, then he hung a right. He hadn't gone a hundred yards before he saw a sign that read Road Ends 50 Feet. That should have put the road's terminal point just around an upcoming curve, but Bolan's GPS showed that the road continued after the turn.

Bolan rounded the curve and found himself in some sort of trashy commune. Old, rusty cars lined both sides of the road; some of them looked drivable, others were just decomposing relics. The cars were parked so tightly on the road that they left just enough room to squeeze through with a motorcycle. Shacks and run-down buildings sat in what appeared to be a cow pasture on the right side of the road, and a few assorted outbuildings in various states of decrepitude littered the hill on the soldier's left. Some of the buildings were clearly abandoned—Bolan could see clean through them because they were missing so many boards and windows—but others showed signs of life inside, a flicker of light behind a dirty window or fresh tracks leading up to the door. Abandoned boats and camper trailers were strewn about the property, keeping the derelict cars, trucks and tractors company.

Contrary to what the sign said, the road continued beyond the flotsam and jetsam that comprised the place. At least it continued in unpaved form. Laguna Road turned into a two-lane dirt trail that curved parallel to Highway One, finally dissecting it when Highway One curved toward the east and wound its way back to Santa Cruz. It didn't look like much of a road, but Bolan was riding the world's biggest trail bike so he continued onward, riding back down the road until it reconnected with Highway One.

Bolan took his time, and when he returned to Santa Cruz, it was dark enough to begin his mission. He turned right on Mission Street, a block west of the Fair Avenue warehouse, then turned left on the next street, parking half a block from the warehouse. He hid his motorcycle behind a semi-truck that was parked along the street and took off his riding suit, revealing the blacksuit underneath. He put the extra magazines for the P90 in pouches snapped on his vest and clipped a couple of M-67 fragmentation grenades and a couple of M-84 flashbangs to his utility belt. He crept between buildings toward the warehouse, jumping fences and avoiding guard dogs along the way. In his left hand he held his sound-supressed Beretta 93-R and in his right he held his Fairbairn-Sykes Fighting Knife. He had to go in quietly, and even the coughing of the Beretta might be too loud.

Bolan crept along the building across the tracks from the warehouse, a Quonset hut made of deeply corrugated metal. The building was constructed of approximately a hundred half-circle steel rings bolted together. The rings were trough-shaped, with outer edges that rose up from a flat center section. When bolted together, the raised sections formed ribs that circled the width of the building. These ribs were spaced roughly sixteen inches apart, and the space between them was about eight inches deep. Bolan put his foot on the brace that held the header for the sliding garage door on the front of the building and kicked himself up onto the roof high enough so that he was able to climb to the top of the building in the trough between the steel ribs.

When he crested the curved steel arch, he scoped out the area. He could see two men behind the building and two in front of it. All of them seemed to be wearing body armor, so Bolan would have to make certain to take head shots. Loud hip-hop music blared from inside the warehouse.

A lone man walked the length of the warehouse. The man turned toward the steel building where the Executioner lay and started to walk directly towards him. Bolan dismissed thoughts of having been discovered when the man below him turned around, unzipped his zipper and began urinating in the dark shadow cast by the Quonset. When Bolan could hear the urine stream dissipating, he slid feet first down the channel between the ribs and landed on the man's shoulders. Wrapping his legs around the man's neck, Bolan grabbed his head and gave it a sharp twist. The man's neck broke with an audible *pop,* and he fell to the ground with Bolan still on top of him.

The Executioner leaped from the man's body and dashed toward the warehouse. He crept toward the rear of the building, sticking close to the edge to remain out of the light cast by the spotlights mounted on top of the warehouse. The music blasting from inside allowed him the freedom to use his suppressed Beretta, so he drew the weapon and set the selector on tri-burst mode.

Bolan peered around the corner. He could smell the marijuana burning in the cigarette that the two men guarding the rear of the building shared. He lined up his sights on the man who had just passed the burning joint to his partner and with a double tap on the trigger he blew off half of the man's head. The partner had closed his eyes while he inhaled the smoke from the joint, and when he opened them, he saw a gaping hole where his buddy's face had been. His eyes got so wide it looked like the skin on his face was going to split, but before he could remove the joint from his lips and shout for help, the Executioner silenced him with another double tap from his Beretta. The man died with the marijuana cigarette still burning between his lifeless lips.

Bolan went to the other side of the building and stuck his head just far enough around the edge to get a glimpse of what was on that side of the building and encountered another man walking straight for him. The man saw the soldier and stopped, sensing something was wrong. Before he had time to process the situation and draw a gun, Bolan lined him up in his sights and pumped two rounds directly into the man's forehead.

The soldier went back behind the warehouse and checked the rear walk-in door. It was unlocked, which made sense, since the two corpses with the smoldering joint were supposed to be guarding it. Bolan cracked the door open and peered inside. A large forklift was backing away from an oversized delivery van and two men were pulling down the overhead rear door of the van's cargo box. At least six other men watched the process, each of them armed with an SAR-21. There were likely more men in the building, but Bolan couldn't see them.

Bolan grabbed one of the flashbangs from his utility belt, pulled the pin, and tossed the bomb toward the van. The movement caught the attention of some of the armed men, but Bolan had the element of surprise on his side. The men simply weren't expecting to be attacked by a black-clad soldier in a Santa Cruz warehouse. Before they could get their minds around what they'd witnessed the M-84 flashbang went off. Bolan shouldered the P90 and rushed into the building while the people inside were still incapacitated from the grenade. Four of the gunmen stood to the left of the van and Bolan sprayed them with a burst of full autofire from the little FN submachine gun. One man fell to the floor, where he remained, motionless. The van took off out the door while the other three dived behind the forklift for cover.

Bolan blasted a short burst into each of the two gunmen on the right of the van, sending multiple rounds directly into the centers of each man's mass. If the rounds didn't hit their hearts, they punched through their spines or other major organs because both men fell, dead or dying.

By this time, the men from the first group had regained their senses and started firing at Bolan. He leaped behind a large crate and crawled around the edge until he reached a point from which he could see where the shots were coming from. The men behind the forklift fired blindly, holding their rifles above the forklift and pulling the triggers without aiming. Their shots went wild, posing a greater threat to the soldier when they ricocheted off something than they did as fired. But the forklift driver had a clear shot at Bolan. He raised a Glock pistol and took direct aim at the Executioner. The man fired and a bullet hit the pavement inches from Bolan's head, sending sharp fragments of concrete into his face.

Bolan snap aimed the P90 and sent a burst into the forklift driver's face. The 5.7 mm bullets were something of a compromise; they were designed to penetrate most soft body armor but in return they lacked the expansion needed to create a large wound channel. But that didn't matter when they penetrated the forklift driver's head. The bullets entered his face, leaving marks that looked like an angry case of chicken pox, and exited through holes that weren't much larger than the entrance holes. But they did their intended job, scrambling the man's reptilian brain stem on their way through.

The whole firefight had lasted less than two minutes, and in that time the driver of the van had started his engine and dropped the transmission into gear. He gunned the engine and the van roared toward the door. Bolan tried to get a shot off after him but return fire from behind the forklift kept him pinned down behind the crate.

It appeared that only three people behind the forklift were firing. Bolan's initial blast must have wounded one of the men more severely than he'd originally thought. He needed to take out all three of them so he could pursue the van, which almost certainly contained the plutonium. Bolan pulled the pin on one of the M-67 fragmentation grenades, counted off three seconds, and hurled the grenade to the far side of the forklift. It exploded before it even hit the ground, shredding all three gunmen in a blast of razor wire.

More gunfire came from the front of the building. The two guards he'd left there had positioned themselves behind a couple of cement-filled steel pipes protruding from the concrete floor, where they were supposed to prevent truck drivers from hitting the tracks for the large overhead doors. Judging from the multicolored paint streaks on the metal pipes, they'd served that purpose more than once. Both men opened fire on the soldier's position. Neither could get a good shot off at Bolan, but in return Bolan was unable to get a clean shot off at either of them.

Not that he needed to kill either of them; what he really needed to do was stop the van carrying the plutonium. He looked at the back door, trying to judge if he could make it there in a dead run before the guards in front of the building shot him. When he looked at the door he saw a head covered with a black nylon do-rag peeking around the door frame. The Executioner put the illuminated yellow dot of his optical sight on the black nylon and squeezed off a single round. The head exploded and another of the BNG gang members fell dead in the doorway. From the commotion outside the door, Bolan could tell that there were others waiting outside.

Bolan weighed his options. He had men coming after him from the front and from behind. He'd reached a détente-like situation with the gunmen in front of him, but the gunmen to his rear would soon realize that they had an advantage over him—if they were careful, they could get aimed shots off at the soldier a lot more easily than he could return fire. He'd have to move to a position that provided a better firing lane to the back door.

To his right stood a small office area that had been built from steel-framed Sheetrock. The area Bolan would have to cross between his current hide and the office offered a clear lane of fire for both guards at the front door. The area to his left didn't offer much more cover—the warehouse was relatively empty—but there were two SUVs parked there. The forklift somewhat shielded the area he'd have to cross from the sight of the gunmen by the front door. If he ran fast enough, Bolan might be able to reach the Cadillac Escalade before the men in front were able to draw a bead on him. He kicked off and sprinted toward the big Cadillac as fast as he could run, a stream of 5.56 mm autofire nipping at his heels the entire way.

From his new position Bolan lobbed an M-67 grenade just outside the rear door, again waiting three seconds before throwing the grenade. The grenade exploded, lacerating everything within its two-meter kill zone. The M-67 didn't kill everyone outside the building, judging by the shrieks of pain that emanated through the door, but it seemed to take the fire out of whoever remained. No one made a further attempt to enter the warehouse from that direction.

Bolan crawled on his belly to the front of the Chevrolet Tahoe. Hiding behind the front driver's side wheel, he leaned over to his right so he could see under the car. From that vantage point he could see one of the guards, or at least he could see the guard's lower body. He couldn't see the man's torso or head.

The Executioner triggered a burst into the man's kneecaps, knocking him to the floor. Bolan held the trigger down, stitching the man's torso as he fell. As soon as the man's head came into Bolan's field of vision, he unleashed another burst from the gun. This time, the bullets exiting the head took a good chunk of the man's skull and gray matter with them.

After taking another glance at the door behind him to make sure that men weren't attacking his six o'clock position, Bolan rushed the final man in the front. Taken by surprise, the man took a moment to respond to the charging wraith in black, and that moment cost him his life. Bolan emptied the P90 into the man's face and replaced the stick magazine as he ran past the man's lifeless corpse and out the front door.

Bolan knew that there still might be men outside, so he went to the front edge of the building and glanced around the corner. Sure enough, he could see an armed man creeping along the wall, moving toward the front of the warehouse. Both men raised their rifles, but Bolan was quicker on the draw and fired off a short burst of rounds, hitting the man in the throat and stitching bullets up across his face.

Bolan didn't see any more men coming so he ran back toward the street, rounded the corner, and didn't stop until he reached his motorcycle. When he approached the bike he looked back and saw two men coming around the corner, heading his way. Bolan raised his gun and looked through the Leupold scope, which he'd turned up to three-power magnification, and saw two of the BNG members running down the street toward his position. He lined up the yellow dot of the reticle on the outline of the closest man's head and triggered a short burst from the P90. The man fell and his buddy dived behind a garbage bin.

Bolan could hear the sirens of approaching emergency vehicles and he knew he had to get out of there. He threw on his riding gear as fast as he could, taking suppressive potshots at the man behind the Dumpster to keep him pinned down. The man took a few wild shots at the soldier, but he wasn't leaving his position to take aimed fire. Bolan let off a long burst, emptying the magazine, and at the same time got on the bike and thumbed the starter.

The engine caught and Bolan gunned the throttle, breaking the rear wheel loose. With his left foot on the ground, Bolan spun the bike around facing away from the gang banger hiding behind the Dumpster and took off after the van. Bolan wheelied the big MW toward Mission Street, leaning forward to keep the oversized dirt bike from flipping over completely. He got the front end down just before he arrived at the intersection. He kept on the throttle but dabbed the rear brake and shifted his weight to the right, putting his right foot down. This made the rear end of the bike step out to the left and he goosed the throttle, sliding around the corner, leaving a big black stripe all the way. He performed the opposite maneuver when he reached Highway One, then got on the throttle as hard as he could. In his mirror he could see multiple vehicles with flashing red lights turning onto Fair Avenue.

The van had a several-minute head start on him and Bolan rode flat out down Highway One, trying to catch the UPO. He reached 130 miles per hour and hoped a deer didn't step out on the road.

After riding down the nearly deserted highway for almost twenty minutes, he spotted the van up ahead. When he approached the vehicle, the overhead door in the cargo box flew open and two men inside opened up on the soldier with SAR-21 rifles. Bolan tried to avoid the flying bullets but one grazed his helmet, snapping his head to the right. Just then several more rounds hit him square in the chest. His head was still reeling from the near miss on his helmet, and the shots in his chest caught him off guard.

The soft armor stopped the 5.56 mm bullets, but the impact knocked the wind out of Bolan and aggravated the broken rib he'd suffered earlier, causing him to lose his grip on the bike's handlebar. Bolan flew off the back of the bike and landed on his back, skidding down the highway. The material in his riding suit was supposed to provide better abrasion resistance than leather at speeds up to one hundred miles per hour. At speeds higher than that the material could melt, leaving the

Executioner's back a bloody, burnt pulp. Bolan had slowed when he came up behind the van, but he hadn't looked at his speedometer.

Apparently he had slowed to under one hundred, because when he came to a stop just before he hit the guardrail on the opposite side of the road, the riding suit saved his skin from being shredded on the pavement. When he stood, the riding suit was damaged beyond repair, but it had protected him from a severe case of road rash. He checked his arms and legs. Everything worked; the only bones that appeared to be broken were the ribs he'd broken earlier.

The bike wasn't so lucky. The big BMW had cartwheeled off the road just before the guardrail next to where the Executioner now stood. He looked down over the cliff. There, more than a hundred feet below him, lay the wrecked motorcycle, smashed to pieces on the railroad track that ran below the road. The headlight was still on, but in the moonlight he could see that there wasn't much left of the mangled remains that resembled a motorcycle. Bolan climbed up to a rocky outcropping above the road on the opposite side where he was out of the sight of any curious passersby and got out his cell phone.

The sun had once again risen over the hills to the east of Monterey by the time Delbert Osborne drove the Executioner to his hotel room. Osborne had learned his lessons well when he'd gone through his blacksuit training at Stony Man Farm and he knew better than to ask Bolan too many questions. Still, the expression on Osborne's face as he drove his Audi S4 back to the hotel let the Executioner know he was curious.

Osborne looked like a good man, and the fact that he'd been through blacksuit training meant that he was a highly trained soldier, but Bolan didn't want to bring him into this unless he absolutely needed help. The problem was that there were still too many unanswered questions and things were happening too fast. Bolan had to be able to react quickly if he learned anything. Though there were times when an extra gun would come in handy, there were even more times when dragging around an extra body would only slow him down.

Bolan hadn't been able to learn anything about the destination of the van. He'd had Kurtzman check the satellite images and the truck had simply disappeared. Kurtzman was able to pull up an image of Bolan closing in on the van just before the occupants had fired on him, very close to where the wrecked BMW lay on the tracks just above the surf of the Pacific Ocean.

When the next satellite had passed over the area twenty-three minutes later, the van had completely disappeared.

Still, this lack of information told the soldier something. The van had to be parked somewhere between San Francisco and Santa Cruz, no farther north than the halfway point between the two cities, and most likely closer to Santa Cruz. There weren't a lot of places to hide a van that size along that route. It was going be difficult, if not impossible, to find the van, but at least it wasn't yet in San Francisco.

He wasn't sure how he was going to proceed from this point. He was kicking around the seeds of an idea that involved kidnapping one of the Team Free Flow staffers, but the problem with that was that he didn't know which staffers were or weren't involved with building the bomb. He wasn't going to take the chance of terrifying some innocent schmuck who didn't have any information to offer. The only people still living that the Executioner knew were involved with the plot were Botros and bin Osman, both of whom were too well guarded to be easily snatched. Even if he could get one of the men, they were hardcase terrorists. Most likely they wouldn't give up the plot even if Bolan resorted to torture, a tool the soldier didn't include in his normal repertoire.

Bolan had arranged for another BMW motorcycle to be delivered to his hotel in Monterey, along with a nearly complete set of riding gear; the only things that survived the crash were his boots. Even his riding gloves had been shredded when the bike hit the rough surface of the highway. But the gear had done its job, and the Executioner's skin was still intact. There wasn't much that he could do until his bike and gear arrived in the morning, so Bolan went up to his room to get some well-deserved sleep.

MUSA BIN OSMAN paced back and forth in the old abandoned turkey shed, his feet wearing the filthy, cracked concrete floor clean. He'd been on edge ever since the stray motorcycle rider had passed through the compound just before dusk. Laguna Road was marked as a dead end, but the trail back down to the highway showed up on GPS programs. As more people equipped their motorcycles with GPS units, the compound had begun to see more and more stray riders passing through.

Randy, the strung-out methamphetamine addict who owned the place, tried to reassure bin Osman. "They're just passing through every now and then. Ain't never caused us no trouble." Bin Osman could barely understand the man; between his thick Okie accent, his habit of mispronouncing every word he spoke and his missing teeth, the words that came out of the man did not sound much like the English language to the Malaysian's ears. But bin Osman wanted to believe the burned-out Okie knew what he was talking about when he said there was nothing to worry about so he let Randy's words calm him.

Randy had let the Filipino gangsters set up a methamphetamine lab in one of his ramshackle outbuildings in return for a steady supply of the highly addictive drug. Now bin Osman had commandeered one of the larger buildings for his own purposes, purposes that might have turned even the BNG against him, had they known what he was building in his makeshift laboratory. He was preparing a nuclear bomb capable of destroying most of San Francisco and taking a good chunk of Oakland with it.

But they didn't know, and they had no need to know. All they knew was that their parent organization in the Philippines had ordered them to assist bin Osman in his assignment and being good soldiers, they were doing just that. So far they'd proved adept at everything except one task—getting rid of the big man posing as a racing fuel salesman.

When bin Osman thought about the tall, dark man who had singlehandedly taken out a crack team of Arab terrorists as well as decimated a truckload of urban gangbangers, he felt cold fear. He'd constructed a plan that no law enforcement agency would ever discover, yet this lone renegade seemed to anticipate his every step. Clearly this man was not associated with any law enforcement agency; the trail of death he left behind was too bloody even for the American CIA to tolerate.

This Cooper had to be either a lone vigilante crusader, which was highly unlikely given his deep resources, or else the member of some supersecret covert operations team. Either that or he was a ghost, some sort of spirit sent to punish bin Osman for his past sins.

Bin Osman chastised himself for thinking such thoughts. Now he was starting to parrot the primitive beliefs of that superstitious savage Jameed Botros. Botros, it seemed, had started to believe that the big man really was the devil.

When the delivery van didn't show up at the allotted time, bin Osman's worry turned to low-grade paranoia. When his cell phone rang, the low-grade paranoia developed into a case of full-blown panic.

"Speak," bin Osman said into the phone.

"He was there," the voice on the other end of the line said. It was Atay, his contact with the Filipino gangsters in San Francisco. Atay had been a high-ranking member of the BNG in the Philippines and had founded the San Francisco branch of the gang. He was now too old to be of much use, but he still wielded enough influence with the gang to get them to work for bin Osman. Atay's cousin Gulay was bin Osman's contact with the Filipino branch of Jemaah Islamiyah. Gulay was one of the top-ranking members of the BNG in the Philippines; he was also a member of Jemaah Islamiyah and completely devoted to the cause of *jihad.*

So far, Atay had proven reliable and resourceful. This was the first time the Filipino had had to contact the Malaysian with bad news.

"*Who* was there?" bin Osman asked, though he already knew the answer.

"The big gas peddler. He killed all but one of my men."

"A more important question might be did your men kill him?"

Atay paused for a moment before answering, irritating bin Osman. His eventual answer didn't do much to placate the Malaysian. "Maybe. I think so."

"What do you mean, 'Maybe'?"

"They shot him while he was riding his motorcycle and they saw the machine go over a cliff and hit the railroad tracks down by the surf. They are sure he was on the bike when it went over the cliff. It was a hundred-foot fall. No man can survive that."

This played into bin Osman's worse fear—that this vengeful creature after him was not a man but some terrible retribution taken human form. "At least tell me we got the material out of the warehouse," bin Osman said.

"We did. It should arrive at the lab any minute."

Just then, the oversized cargo van pulled into the compound. Bin Osman's men directed it inside the turkey shed, which was barely high enough at its crest to accept the tall van. Bin Osman felt relief wash over him like a cleansing shower, but at the same time the intense adrenaline rush he'd felt left him nauseous and he had to fight to keep the bile down.

Bin Osman ordered one of his men to take an old Jeep CJ that Randy owned down to the Coastal Highway and make certain this Cooper was dead once and for all. The Jeep was one of the few vehicles on the compound that ran, and it was ideal for navigating the dirt track that constituted the back route to the highway.

The Jeep arrived on the scene just as Cooper got into a car and drove off. Bin Osman's man tried to pursue the car, but it was a high-performance European sedan and the driver seemed to know how to exploit the car's formidable capabilities. He drove at a pace that made it impossible for the underpowered old Jeep to keep up. Bin Osman's man kept the accelerator pedal of the Jeep to the floor while he watched the taillights of the Audi disappear in the distance. When the Audi was out of sight, he called bin Osman on his cell phone.

"The big man's not dead yet," the Jeep driver told his boss. "He just got into a car and drove back toward Santa Cruz."

When bin Osman hung up he once again felt a wave of nausea ripple through his digestive tract and he fought to keep from vomiting. When his stomach had settled down, he made another phone call.

"What is it?" Botros said into the line, obviously unhappy about being awakened in the wee hours of the morning.

"I need you to act," bin Osman said to the Saudi. "I need you to send your best man to kill Cooper in his hotel room. He should arrive in about ninety minutes. This must be done by first light. Do not fail me."

The Executioner knew immediately that someone had been in his room. He'd stuffed a small folded piece of a matchbook cover between the door and the frame, and it now lay on the floor in front of his door. He'd asked not to receive any maid service and so far no maid had entered his room.

Bolan walked back to the elevator area and punched a speed-dial button on his cell phone. "How far away from the hotel are you?" he asked Osborne.

"I've just pulled out onto the street."

"Would you mind pulling back in and coming up to Room 312? I have a situation."

"I'm on my way."

The Executioner approached the door to his room as silently as possible and stopped outside to listen for movement from within the room. He heard nothing, but the sixth sense he'd developed over years of fighting told him someone was inside. He didn't want to chance having stray bullets flying through the paper-thin walls and killing innocent travelers in adjoining rooms. It was a distinct possibility even with his 9 mm Beretta, so he drew the Fairbairn-Sykes knife from the leg sheath he wore over his blacksuit and prepared to enter the room. He inserted his key card. The lights on the lock turned green, and he threw open the door while at the same time spinning away from the doorway. No bullets came.

Bolan entered the room and glanced into the bathroom to his left. He didn't see anyone, but the shower curtain was closed. He'd left it open when he'd showered the previous evening on purpose—he liked to have any space where he slept as open to view as possible. Others might consider him paranoid, but it was such careful consideration and situational awareness that had helped him stay alive all these years. That, along with a fair amount of luck.

With one eye on the bathroom door, Bolan backed into the main part of the room and scanned the sleeping area. The drapes were drawn, but there wasn't enough room for even the thinnest human being to hide between the drapes and the windows. The only area in the main room where an assailant could hide was under the bed, but Bolan knew that was impossible because the bed was on a pedestal and there was no space under it. That meant if someone was in the room, he or she was hiding behind the shower curtain.

The soldier crept back to the bathroom, trying to figure out a way to capture the person hiding behind the shower curtain alive. Perhaps he might know where bin Osman's men had taken the plutonium. He reached around and turned the switch that operated the ceiling fan, creating noise in the room that would cover his movements and stood back from the door. He pulled an extendable baton from his utility belt, extended it to full length, and with his left hand he used the baton to open the curtain. In his right hand he held the razor-sharp Fairbairn-Sykes.

He'd pulled the curtain about six inches by the time the figure inside lunged out at him. The man swung a dagger down toward the Executioner's clavicle. Bolan swung his right hand across the attacker's right hand and knocked his aim off so that his knife skimmed along Bolan's left arm. The blade cut through the soldier's blacksuit and bit into his skin, opening a gash from his bicep to the middle of his forearm before he could completely knock the attacker's hand away. Bolan felt his arm getting wet with blood, but he could see it was only a superficial wound.

Bolan swung the metal sap in his left hand across the attacker's jaw, knocking him backward into the shower wall. The man bounced off the wall and lunged toward Bolan, but this time the Executioner was better prepared and had assumed a proper fighting stance. Once again he slapped away the blade that the attacker thrust at him, but this time he did so with his left hand, leaving his right hand free to counterattack with his own blade. He sliced the knife down across the attacker's right arm, opening up a much deeper wound than the attacker had opened up in Bolan's left arm.

Right away the Executioner could see that the wound was too deep. The attacker had twisted his arm when Bolan had knocked it aside so that the underside of the arm was exposed. He'd filleted the arm, opening up a six-inch stretch of the main artery. The man fell back into the tub, blood spraying from his arm like a split fire hose. Bolan hoped to keep the man alive because he wanted to question him, but one look at his face told the soldier that he was already going into shock. He would soon be dead. "Where is the plutonium?" Bolan asked the dying man.

"*Allahu Akbar,*" the man whispered, his draining blood filling the bathtub. They were the last words the man would ever speak.

Bolan grabbed a towel to stop the blood from his own wounded arm and wrapped the cut area. He heard a knock at the door. He took quick glance through the peephole and saw Osborne. He hurried to the door and let the ex-cop into the room, closing the door behind him.

"S'up?" the retired San Francisco detective asked. Bolan pointed toward the bathroom. Osborne stepped into the room and came out a moment later. "Holy shit," he said.

"That about sums it up," Bolan said.

"You're bleeding," Osborne said, pointing at the Executioner's left arm.

The soldier examined the wound. It was shallow, but it was bleeding profusely. He'd have to tape it up or he'd be a bloody mess.

"Who's that?"

"I think I saw him working in the Team Free Flow garage on Thursday. I'm pretty sure he's a Saudi."

"What are we going to do with him?"

"Good question," the soldier replied. He thought a bit and said, "I think we should take him back where he came from."

THE EXECUTIONER WALKED THROUGH the open overhead door of the Team Free Flow garage complex, took out his Beretta 93-R, and said, "I want to see Botros right now."

The mechanic nearest the office area drew a Glock from a waistband holster but before he had it halfway up Bolan grabbed the crew member, put the Beretta to his temple, and said, "Tell your boss to get out here."

"He doesn't speak English," another crew member said.

Bolan turned his aim on the English speaker. "Then you tell your boss to get out here. Now."

"I cannot do that," the mechanic said.

"Well I can put a bullet through your melon. Get him out here."

By this time the man was nearly in tears. "I cannot get him because he is not here."

Bolan looked at the man to see if he was telling the truth. He showed nothing but fear.

"Where'd he go?" Bolan asked.

"I do not know."

"Listen, I've had a really bad night," Bolan said. "I'm in no mood for games. Tell me where I can find Botros."

"I genuinely do not know," the man, who was nearly hysterical, said between giant sobs.

Bolan pressed the barrel of the gun against the man's head. "Take a guess," he said.

"All I know is he went somewhere between Santa Cruz and San Francisco. Where exactly, I do not know."

Bolan shouted to everyone in the room, "Listen up. I have something for your boss." He whistled and a car engine started outside the door. Osborne backed his car in through the door and popped open the trunk. Bolan reached in and pulled out something wrapped in a blood-splattered shower curtain. He unfurled the shower curtain and the body of the man who attacked him in his hotel room rolled to the floor. The man's blood had completely drained into the bathtub and his skin was a ghastly grayish white, but the men recognized their comrade.

"I don't want this one," the Executioner said. "It's broken."

While the members of Team Free Flow stared at the gruesome sight of their dead comrade, Bolan jumped in the car and Osborne tore out of the garage, all four fat tires of the Audi twisting up a noisy cloud of smoking rubber.

"HE WHAT?" Botros couldn't believe what the man on the other end of the cell phone had just told him. "Is he insane?" He paused while the man back at Laguna Seca asked him what they should do with the body.

"Wrap him up in the shower curtain and throw him in the Dumpster in the back. Of course they will find him, but by then we'll be on a jet heading back to Saudi Arabia, and the American authorities will have much greater problems than a body in a Dumpster." He paused again while the man calling from the garage protested disposing of his brethren in such an undignified manner.

"He is a martyr," Botros said. "He has given his life for *jihad.* He is guaranteed passage to Heaven. We should be so fortunate."

Botros projected bravery to his man back in Laguna Seca, but in reality he feared he may very well end up a martyr himself and he felt anything but fortunate. He'd begun to believe that this tall stranger with no background had sprung from the bowels of Hell, a demon come to bring Botros back to Hell with him. He'd exercised bad judgment by expressing this thought to bin Osman, after which he'd been chastised for being a superstitious savage. But he suspected bin Osman had developed a healthy fear of this strange man himself.

Of a more immediate concern was telling his superior he'd failed to kill the big devil. Depending on bin Osman's temperament at the moment, Cooper may not even get the chance to drag Botros down to Hell. If bin Osman decided his failure was unacceptable, the man would bring Hell to Botros before he even died. Many young boys torture insects and small animals, but thankfully they outgrow it. Bin Osman was one of the terrifying few who hadn't; rather, he'd graduated to ever larger and more challenging creatures to torture, ultimately settling on human beings as his subject of choice.

Unfortunately for Botros, bin Osman was not in a very good mood. Gunthar Maurstad, the scientist from Los Alamos whom he had coerced into assembling the nuclear device he planned to detonate in San Francisco the following evening, was stalling.

"Bring out the woman," bin Osman ordered one of the Saudis that Botros had assigned to help assemble the bomb. A moment later, the man pushed a female figure, her hands bound behind her back, her feet shackled together and a canvas hood over her head, into the filthy, decaying turkey shed that served as their makeshift laboratory. "Secure her to the chair." He pointed to a wooden chair that he'd had bolted to the floor.

"Dr. Maurstad, you are trying my patience. Do not think that I can't see through what you are trying to do. Believe me when I tell you it will not work. Did you think I was joking when I said that if you did not cooperate, I would torture your family?"

Maurstad lunged toward bin Osman, but he hadn't gone three feet before several Saudis subdued him.

"You have had ample opportunity to prevent this from happening, but my patience has worn thin. The time has come for me to show you that I am serious." Bin Osman produced a curved dagger and began cutting the bag over the woman's head from the back to the front, slicing the heavy canvas with the sharp dagger as if it were tissue paper. The woman tried to scream, but a gag filled her mouth.

"Remember, everything I do to your wife, I will then do to your daughter if you do not cooperate.

"Nancy!" Maurstad shrieked to his wife, but was cut off in mid syllable by a fist into his jaw.

"I regret having to do this," bin Osman lied—in reality he was excited about torturing Maurstad's wife.

Bin Osman grabbed the front of the woman's dress, which had looked elegant and expensive on the morning that his men had kidnapped the Maurstad family as they returned home from church but now looked like a filthy collection of rags. Bin Osman sliced down the front of the dress. The opportunity to practice his art came far too seldom these days. As a member of Malaysia's elite upper class, bin Osman had been able to prey on Malaysia's impoverished lower classes as a young man, but a concerted effort to build the nation's middle class depleted the ranks of potential victims for the twisted man to torture. While studying abroad, bin Osman had sublimated his urge to torture by engaging in date rape at every possibility, but he'd had to curtail even that mild diversion as he'd rose in the ranks of the business world.

When he'd had his religious awakening and devoted his life to *jihad,* he once again gained access to subjects on which to practice his art and he thanked Allah for every opportunity to do so. These days it was the closest thing he got to sexual release.

Maurstad babbled, "All right, I'll do it. I'll finish putting together the explosive device. It will be ready to transport by midday tomorrow."

Bin Osman was glad that the man had seen the light, pleased that he would do his part in implementing the Malaysian's plan, but he felt cheated of his fun with the Maurstad women. He would have to find some other means of relieving the tension that had built up in his groin.

Maurstad had returned to work and bin Osman had left

Nancy Maurstad tied up in the center of the room in order to motivate the scientist to do the job. When Jameed Botros entered the building, bin Osman could tell from the look on the Saudi's face that he wasn't going to like what Botros was about to say. Bin Osman decided to make the task as difficult as possible.

"You have come to tell me that your man has taken care of this mad American, correct?" he asked Botros.

"Not quite," Botros said.

"I thought you sent your best man to kill him."

"I did."

"And the man failed. What does he have to say for himself?"

"Nothing," Botros said. "Cooper just dumped his body in the middle of the garage complex."

"He what?"

"He drove a car into the garage complex and dumped our man's body on the floor. He'd been knifed and there wasn't a drop of blood left in him when the American threw him on the floor."

"How is this possible?" bin Osman asked. "Did your men simply sit around and allow this to happen?"

"No. One of my men attempted to shoot the American."

"How did that work out?" bin Osman asked, though he suspected he knew the answer.

"Cooper pulled his gun faster."

Bin Osman gave the Saudi a look that he knew would make the man squirm in his skin. Who was this man who hounded his every step? He was no law enforcement officer—he killed with too much impunity to be associated with any law enforcement organization. And he was no soldier, at least not in any Western military organization. Even the Russians didn't operate as recklessly as this man. He had heard Botros call him *Iblis,* the fire demon, the Islamic equivalent of Satan. He had written off the Saudi's fear of the American as the barbaric superstition of a primitive, but now he wasn't so sure.

Regardless, Botros would have to pay for his failure, though that payment would have to wait until after they'd accomplished their mission. Bin Osman needed the Saudis to complete the mission, and they were so close now he could smell success. Just another day and a half and the Islamic revolution would step up to an entirely new level.

Bolan and Osborne drank coffee in the soldier's hotel room, waiting for Kurtzman to get back to them. Osborne took a drink from his cup and winced. "You like your coffee on the strong side," he observed.

"This? I take it you never had the coffee when you took your blacksuit training." If Osborne had tasted the sludge Kurtzman called coffee, anything else would seem like brown water.

"No, I never did."

Bolan and Osborne had spent hours cleaning the bloody mess in the bathroom and had just returned from dumping the assassin's body in the Team Free Flow garage complex. Bolan had sketched in the details of his mission to the blacksuit and Osborne offered his services to help the Executioner find the plutonium. Bolan studied the man. So far he'd proven to have the strength needed to do this sort of work, both physically and emotionally, and Bolan's instincts told him the blacksuit was someone who could be trusted.

"There is something you might be able to do," Bolan told Osborne, "but it could be dangerous."

"Worse than what we've already done?"

"Much worse. If I need you for the job I have in mind, that'll mean I've failed to find the plutonium and you'll be sitting on top of a high-powered nuclear device. That would make you the last line of defense between life continuing in America as usual and something that could very well resemble Armageddon. The sensible thing for you to do would be to hightail it to someplace about two thousand miles from here."

"You're talking about my city, Cooper. I refuse to abandon her in her time of need."

Bolan looked at the man. Of course the soldier knew Osborne would not abandon his city, but Bolan had wanted to hear it from his own mouth. "Okay, I need you to go back to the city and remain ready to stop the Free Flow people from detonating the bomb if something happens to me in the next couple of days. For now you might want to go home and rest."

"It's been a long night," Osborne admitted. "It's been awhile since I pulled an all-nighter like this."

"I wish I could say the same," Bolan said. "I'll contact you as soon as I know anything."

"I'll say one thing about you, Cooper," Osborne said. "You don't screw around."

Osborne had barely shut the door when Bolan's phone rang. "What did you find out, Bear?" Bolan asked.

"You're not going to like what I've got to say, Striker."

"I don't like anything about this situation, so why should this be any different?"

"I've narrowed the possible destinations of the van down to twelve locations."

"Just twelve, huh?"

"I can't tell if you're being sarcastic or if you're just tired," Kurtzman said.

"Both. Can you send the locations to my GPS unit?"

"No problem."

"How about my new wheels?" Bolan asked.

"Problem," Kurtzman said. "I wasn't able to get another bike like the last one. In fact, there wasn't a motorcycle to be rented in northern California, so I had to buy one."

"What did you get?"

"I think you'll like it. It's another BMW, an F800GS. It's down some on power, but the top speed is almost identical because the bike is lighter and the handling is much better, both on- and off-road. You can actually take this one into the dirt."

"When will it be here?" the soldier asked.

"Within the hour."

"Good. I have a lot of territory to cover if I'm going to check out all twelve locations." Bolan wasn't looking forward to trying to scout a dozen locations, but at the moment he really didn't have any other choice—he had to find that plutonium.

"I've got one more piece of information that might help you. We've lost one of our top scientists from Los Alamos." Kurtzman referred to the Los Alamos National Laboratory, meaning only one thing—someone might have access to one of the nation's most capable nuclear scientists.

"What do you mean 'lost' him?" Bolan asked.

"I mean we lost him. He and his family have just disappeared. He was coming home from church with his wife and daughter and they all disappeared. We found their car abandoned between the church and their home."

"Any chance he defected?"

"Highly unlikely," Kurtzman said. "He checks out solid. And there appears to be signs of struggle in the vehicle. The wife left her purse and the daughter left her iPod."

"Not good. If he was kidnapped, any idea who grabbed him?"

"We do. We think it may have been MS-13." MS-13 was a street gang that had started out in El Salvador and spread to the American Southwest. In recent years they'd been responsible for a crime wave that had swept through Arizona and New Mexico.

"Aren't the BNG and MS-13 mortal enemies?" Bolan asked.

"They seem to have formed some kind of truce and they've been working together in a few different cities. It makes sense that they'd eventually link up. The Filipino street gangs tend to have close ties with the Hispanic street gangs."

"What's the scientist's name?"

"Gunthar Maurstad," Kurtzman said. "His wife is Nancy and his daughter is Mareebeth, with three E's."

"Three E's?" Bolan asked.

"Maurstad's from Germany, but his wife's people are hillbillies from northern Arkansas," Kurtzman said. "They can't help it."

"How old is the daughter?"

"Six."

"You think bin Osman has them?"

"It could be a coincidence," Kurtzman said, "but I don't think so. This doesn't appear to be a typical kidnapping. There's been no demand for ransom, and nothing was stolen from the vehicle."

It may have been a coincidence, but the soldier's instincts told him that Kurtzman was probably right.

11

Because the Laguna Seca track was the westernmost track on the MotoGP circuit, the time difference with the rest of the world was problematic so the qualifying session was moved up from the usual noon start to nine in the morning.

Eddie Anderson stretched on the ground in the pit area beside his motorcycle. He wanted to be as limber as possible for the session ahead. By the time he was ready to ride out onto the track, his head was completely clear of any thoughts not pertaining to the job at hand. His brother had owned Laguna Seca, both in his American Motorcyclist Association racing days and during his brief but spectacular MotoGP career. He'd set the lap record on his 990 cc bike, a time that no one thought would ever be beaten since the switch to 800 cc bikes.

Maybe his brother's record would never be beaten, but Eddie felt he could do it. His bike was fast enough, and everything just felt right. He even thought Darrick would want him to break the record. In some strange way he felt like his brother was there on the track with him.

Eddie rode out on the track and opened up the throttle. He'd hit two hundred miles per hour by Turn One and he braked hard for the Andretti Hairpin. He circled the difficult corner perfectly, hitting his apex points exactly where he wanted. He flew through Turns Three and Four as if they weren't even corners and took Turn Five faster than he ever had before. And he was still warming up his tires, preparing for his really fast lap. He hit his braking points perfectly for Turn Six and rocketed up the hill toward the Corkscrew, the infamous downhill left-right chicane. When he exited the bottom turn he felt like he was piloting a low-flying airplane instead of an earthbound motorcycle. He rocketed through Rainey Curve, completely forgetting the previous day's unpleasantness, and set himself up for the deceivingly slow Turn Ten. He hit his braking markers perfectly once again as he approached Turn Eleven—always his most difficult corner—and hit his apex spot on.

After a couple of more laps, he was ready to start turning in some hot laps. He rode every lap a bit better than the last and before he'd even completely broken in his soft qualifying tires he was approaching his brother's record lap time. When his tires finally came into their own, he rode the most blazingly fast laps of his entire career. When the dust had settled, he turned in a best lap that shattered his brother's record by almost a second. While part of him felt guilty about taking away one of his brother's proudest moments, he could almost hear Darrick cheering for him with the rest of the crowd.

In the post-qualifying press conference Eddie, who had never been at a loss for words, choked up. The press had come to rely on his colorful statements to provide provocative pull quotes in their stories. They bombarded him with questions, but Anderson knew that if he tried to speak, he would burst into tears. Finally he managed to say, "I did it for Darrick," and he walked out of the building.

EDDIE ANDERSON was supposed to stick close to the garage area throughout the racing weekend, but after the press conference he felt he had to get away from the masses of people at the track.

He put on his street helmet and street-riding leathers, climbed aboard his Ducati motorcycle and rode away from the track.

Anderson turned left at the gate and headed east on the Monterey Salinas Highway. Traffic was backed up for miles coming into the track, but since the races were just beginning hardly anyone was leaving the track and Anderson had the road away from the track almost to himself. He loved his motorcycle, a gift from his employers at Ducati. It was like an overgrown, overpowered dirt bike. It wasn't the most comfortable machine for long trips, but it was crazy maneuverable and wicked fun on a twisty road. Perhaps its only real drawback was that the rearview mirrors were virtually useless, especially when the big twin-cylinder engine revved up and started buzzing them with its throbbing vibration.

Normally this wasn't a serious problem; a rider only needed to know that something was behind him or her and that he or she needed to be careful. It only became a problem when the person behind was a law enforcement official and the rider was having a little too much fun on a public road. Or in the case of Eddie Anderson, leaving the Mazda Raceway, if the person behind was a Filipino gangbanger who had been hired to kidnap him and take him to a Malaysian terrorist with a perverted need to torture him.

Several BNG members in a modified Mitsubishi Evo tailed Anderson down the Monterey Salinas Highway. After another failed attempt to dispatch Cooper, bin Osman had redoubled his efforts to eliminate the meddlesome young Anderson brother and had a team of BNG members watching him at all times. The attempted kidnapping on Thursday seemed not to affect the kid and he'd continued to squawk about the death of his brother. He'd even mentioned him at the press conference after his record-breaking qualifying ride. Bin Osman didn't seem to be able to clip the loose thread that was the marauding American, but he could certainly handle this boy.

After riding a short way Anderson turned right and rode south on the Laureles Grade Road, a twisty, empty road that wound its way toward the little bedroom community of Carmel Valley. He hadn't noticed the bright red sport compact following him so far, but he rode in such a spirited manner his pursuers assumed he was making a break for it and drove the Mitsubishi so fast its intercooled turbocharger glowed red hot. In reality this was how Anderson always rode motorcycles; his idea of a relaxing pace differed radically from what most riders considered relaxing—for Eddie Anderson, a hundred miles per hour felt so slow that he thought he was going backward, which is why he didn't ride on the street much.

The Mitsubishi was one of the few cars with the power needed to keep up with the Ducati on such a twisty road, but the driver of the car was no match for Anderson when it came to skill. Without effort Anderson kept so much distance between himself and the overachieving sport compact car that he never even realized he was being followed. Before the trailing car reached the halfway point the driver had called ahead for help.

Anderson rode as hard as he dared, watching for deer and cars coming out of hidden driveways, enjoying the freedom of being away from all the pressure of the track. He slowed to a sane pace when he rode into the more populated area around Carmel Valley, but he was still going too fast when a low-rider pickup truck backed out in front of him from La Rancheria

Road. The vehicle took him completely by surprise because there was no reason for the pickup to be going backward.

At least Anderson couldn't imagine a reason for the truck to be backing up, but the driver had a very good reason for his aberrational driving—he wanted to make Anderson crash.

Anderson got on the brakes hard, but the dual-sport tires on his motorcycle lacked the grip of the super sticky race tires he was used to riding on and he broke both wheels loose. He missed the pickup, but in the process he low-sided the bike and it slid in front of the front bumper, Anderson following it as he skidded along the pavement in his ventilated leather riding suit.

By the time he'd come to a stop, the driver of the pickup truck and a passenger had run over to where he was sprawled on the road. Anderson assumed they'd come to help him until he saw the Glocks in each of their hand.

"Get up," the driver shouted. Before Anderson could stand, the Mitsubishi had pulled onto the scene.

"Get in the car," the driver commanded, waving toward the open back door with his Glock. Before he could comply, two men jumped out of the back seat and slammed the motorcycle racer into the back of the car. One of the passengers jumped in one door and the other jumped in the opposite door. Fitting three average-sized Americans in the back seat of the Mitsubishi would have been physically impossible, but the two men who had jumped out were slight of stature, and Anderson's morphotype was about as far from the average American's as possible. Still, it was a tight fit and the two Filipinos pinned Anderson in the seat so he couldn't move.

He watched through the windshield as the other members of the crew threw his motorcycle into the back of the pickup.

They didn't want to leave behind any sign that something had happened to the young American rider. When the bike was in the pickup, both the car and truck left the scene. Anderson tried to imagine how he might exit the scene himself, but with one Glock poking him in each side of his rib cage, he knew that wasn't going to be easy.

BOLAN WAS READY to start looking for the plutonium when he noticed Eddie Anderson changing and then riding away from the track. That worried him, but not nearly as much as when he noticed that Anderson was being followed by four men in a Mitsubishi sport compact with a loud coffee-can muffler and an oversized carbon-fiber rear wing. When the car drove past him, Bolan saw a distinct question-mark tattooed on the driver's arm. He hated to take time away from hunting for the plutonium, but he knew he couldn't let Anderson meet the same fate as his brother.

The BNG crew in the Mitsubishi were so focused on following Anderson that they didn't notice Bolan's motorcycle tailing them. When they turned right on Laureles Grade Road, the Executioner was about ten car lengths back. He hadn't expected either Anderson or the BNG members to take off so quickly once they got off the main highway, but by the time he turned the corner and was heading south, Anderson was nowhere to be seen and the Mitsubishi was disappearing around a bend almost half a mile ahead of him.

Bolan rode as hard as he could to try to catch up with the Ducati and Mitsubishi, but Anderson's riding skills were so advanced and the Ducati so fast that Bolan couldn't catch up to him even though he held the throttle to the stop for most of the way down to Carmel Valley. When both bikes were ridden by riders of equal skill, the Ducati Hypermotard was one of the few motorcycles capable of outrunning the BMW on a tight, twisty road like Laureles Grade Road. As good as he was, Bolan's riding skills were a long way from equal to those of Eddie Anderson, who many people thought might turn out to be the greatest motorcycle racer of all time.

The Mitsubishi was just as hard to catch. Bolan rode an extremely capable bike for the type of road, but it was no match for a high-powered car with a well-tuned suspension and sticky gumball racing tires. It was a simple matter of physics; a vehicle's ability to negotiate a curve depends in large part on the amount of rubber connected to the road. Not only did the Mitsubishi have four tires to the motorcycle's two, but because of the size and flat profile of the tires, each of the four had a bigger contact patch on the pavement than the rounded tires of Bolan's bike. Bolan soon lost contact with both Anderson and the gangbangers.

Just as he pulled into Carmel Valley, the Executioner saw the Mitsubishi turn right onto Carmel Valley Road heading toward Monterey. A red pickup with wide, low-profile tires seemed to be following closely. Anderson was nowhere to be seen. When Bolan got to the intersection of Laureles Grade Road and La Rancheria Road he saw fresh skid marks that looked like a motorcycle had just crashed. On the side of the road he spotted a broken black plastic hand protector and a broken piece of red plastic. It looked like the fork-seal guard from Anderson's Ducati. He saw no other evidence of a bike or a rider.

The pickup, Bolan thought. The bike might be in the pickup. That meant that if Anderson was still alive, he might be in either the car or the pickup. Bolan cranked on the throttle and rode to the Stop sign at the intersection of Carmel Valley Road and Laureles Grade Road. Looking right, he saw the pickup and car disappearing over the crest of a hill. Bolan jammed on the throttle and slid the bike around until he was facing west, toward Monterey and the ocean, and cranked the throttle wide open once he was straightened out.

Bolan rode full-out through most of the little bedroom suburb of Carmel Valley. When he got the vehicles back in sight, he eased up, not wanting to draw the attention of the gangbangers or the local constabulary. Using other vehicles for cover so that the gangbangers wouldn't spot him, he followed the vehicles to Carmel-by-the-Sea, then back to Monterey, through town and up the Coastal Highway toward Santa Cruz. Because there were so many motorcycles going to and coming from the racetrack, the soldier's glowing headlight was just one of thousands on the road and the gangbangers never noticed they were being followed. The four-wheeled vehicles were forced to move at a crawl while Bolan could position himself pretty much wherever he wanted thanks to the mobility of his motorcycle. He continued to follow the vehicles through Santa Cruz. Out of town just a couple of miles beyond where he'd crashed the big BMW the night before, the two vehicles turned right onto Laguna Road.

Bolan rode past the turnoff, and when he was out of sight of the intersection, he made a U-turn and headed back. Once again he rode past the main drive up to the derelict compound he'd spotted earlier. He knew it was the only possible place they could be taking Anderson. When he got to the back route to the compound he turned off the highway. When he was about a half mile from the building site, he rode off the road and down into a shallow gully. He removed his riding gear, revealing digital camo-pattern Marine MARPAT fatigues. In the broad daylight, his blacksuit would have been almost as visible as a neon-pink leotard, but the Marines had a digital desert camo pattern that was perfect for the dry hills north of Santa Cruz. Under his marine blouse he wore the soft body armor he'd had on when he'd crashed his motorcycle. It had taken a beating and its integrity was questionable if someone shot him in the exact same spots he'd been hit before, but it was better than nothing.

He stowed his riding gear in the top box, equipped himself with the P90, extra magazines for both the little FN subgun as well as for his Beretta and Desert Eagle, and clipped more grenades to his utility belt. They'd come in handy on this mission.

When he was ready for battle, he leaned his bike against a dirt bank and threw some sage brush over it for camouflage.

Bolan crept through the brush alongside the road, plotting a course that would take him into the compound in an area not likely to be heavily guarded. He emerged from the brush in a clearing near what looked like a lived-in trailer home. He crept to the rear of the trailer and raised his head just high enough to see into the window of the master bedroom, or what passed for the master bedroom in the rusted, filthy little receptacle of broken humanity.

Broken humanity was exactly what he saw inside the trailer. A nude woman lay sprawled on the bed, her body so emaciated that he could see the outline of her hipbone through her skin. Her body fat was so low that her breasts, if she had ever had them, had virtually disappeared, leaving just loose skin with brown nipples. The space between her thighs had to be three inches wide. The only thing that kept the Executioner from thinking he was looking at a corpse was that he could see her bony chest rising and falling as she breathed.

A man sat on the bed, banging a needle in his arm. Judging from his equally emaciated state, the syringe must have contained methamphetamine. Judging from the smell that permeated the compound, a tub full of meth cake was cooling somewhere close by.

Bolan made his way to the outbuilding closest to the trailer. Unlike many of the outbuildings that comprised the compound, this one had glass in the windows. It also had a lock on the door. Bolan pulled a small, flat bar from his utility belt and pried the lock latch free from the door. The five screws holding it popped from the rotting wood on the doorframe with such ease that the soldier really didn't need to use the pry bar. With his sound-suppressed Beretta leading the way, the soldier entered the building, spinning around to make certain it was empty.

It was empty of people, but it did contain all the equipment a person needed to have a medium-scale methamphetamine manufacturing operation. An old claw-foot bathtub sat to one side, and inside a sheet of meth cake cooled, waiting to be processed. The stench of the chemicals was so powerful that Bolan had to exit the building as quickly as possible.

He pulled a small pair of binoculars from a pouch on his utility belt and scanned the compound, looking for a building large enough for Botros and bin Osman to use for storing the van carrying the plutonium. Across the road he saw what he was looking for—a long, low turkey shed, the only large building in the compound without a caved-in roof. The corrugated-steel building was about ninety feet long and about fifteen feet high at the peak of the roof. Green skylight panels ran from the gables to the peak every ten feet, and the sides were covered with louvered ventilation panels spaced out at similar ten-foot intervals. Three-foot tall, fifteen-foot wide wooden doors ran along the bottom of the building. When turkeys had been raised there, they would be opened to let the turkeys move in and out of the shed.

In addition to being intact, the building stood out for a couple of other reasons. First, a brand-new power pole stood in front of the building, with a halogen yard light mounted atop it and thick, new power lines ran from the top of the pole to the turkey shed. It was the only building in the compound that had new lines running to it. Any of the other out buildings that had power lines running to them had old, decaying lines with insulation that was flaking off in big chunks. Excluding the new line running to the turkey shed, there wasn't a power line on the place that looked less than fifty years old.

The second feature that set the building apart was the front door. A brand-new overhead door stood in center of the building's facade. The large door looked as if it cost more than the building was worth. From the brand-new corrugated steel that flanked either side of the door, it appeared that the building had been equipped with a pair of sliding doors until fairly recently. The door was closed, but judging from the glow coming from the skylights, lights burned inside the building.

Bolan scanned the area through his binoculars. He was looking for signs of life. He saw several derelict vehicles had been strategically placed around the building. Upon close inspection Bolan made out a man hiding within each of them. Inside one of the vehicles, a rusted Chevrolet Caprice from the late 1970s, he saw the short barrel of an SAR-21 bullpup combat rifle poking up from between the legs of the man inside.

Bolan still had the binoculars to his eyes trying to count the number of sentries guarding the building when he heard the fast-moving low growl coming at him from behind. He dropped the binoculars and swung around just as the guard dog lunged through the air toward his jugular. Years of experience had honed the Executioner's reflexes to a point where he reacted before his brain could shoot the synapses needed to process a dangerous situation and when he grabbed the dog by the side of its head and swung it to the ground, he did so on pure instinct.

The dog squirmed and lunged back up at Bolan. Bolan deflected it with his left arm, ripping open the dressed wound from the previous night's knife fight. With his right arm he again grabbed the side of the dog's head and twisted it away from his body, preventing the animal from locking its powerful jaws in his flesh. This time Bolan followed the dog down and slammed his knee into its neck. The dog tried to squirm free, thrashing its legs, neck and head back and forth. The dog's sharp claws slashed through Bolan's fatigues and tore into his skin, but he held firm and kept the dog pinned. Grabbing its head with both hands, careful to steer clear of the lethal mouth, the Executioner twisted the beast's head with all his strength, pinning the neck as hard as he possibly could with his knee and lower leg. Finally he heard the loud sound of the dog's neck breaking and the thrashing stopped, replaced by the spastic twitching of the animal's death throes.

"Now why'd you have to go and kill my dog," a voice behind the soldier said. Bolan turned to find himself staring down the barrel of a sawed-off Mossberg 500 12-gauge pump shotgun. Behind it stood the ghastly scarecrow of a man he'd seen in the trailer. The man stood about four yards away from the soldier, far enough for the pattern from the short-barreled shot gun to hit the body armor and take Bolan's head off at the same time. The man had the drop on Bolan and there was nothing he could do.

JAMEED BOTROS stared at the bloated, disfigured carcass that just a short while before had been Nancy Maurstad. After Gunthar Maurstad had finished assembling the nuclear explosive device, bin Osman had tortured the man's wife to death, just to demonstrate what would happen to the man's daughter should the device fail to detonate. Botros was a hard man and he had seen much violence in his fifty-some years of life, but he had never seen anything like this. Bin Osman clearly knew what he was doing, cutting very slowly and keeping the woman alive far longer than Botros would have ever thought possible. What was left of her looked more like a butchered hog than the remains of a human being.

It was typical of bin Osman to have his fun and then leave Botros to clean up his mess. The arrogant Malaysian considered himself to be above Botros and his men. Botros loathed bin Osman almost as much as he loathed the decadent Westerners whose entire world he and bin Osman were in the final stages of permanently upending. The fact that he couldn't do this without the Malaysian's help was the only thing that kept Botros from slitting the swine's throat. As he looked at the bloody mess tied to the chair in the middle of the building, he admitted to himself that a healthy amount of fear also kept him from disposing of bin Osman.

Botros ordered his men to clean up the mess and remove the large woman's carcass. He would have preferred to abandon this site altogether, kill that miserable addict who owned the place along with his harlot of a wife and get back to the racetrack, but bin Osman had left the Maurstad girl tied up in the cleaning room at the rear entrance of the building. He'd kept her alive in part to motivate her father to activate the nuclear device once they placed it in the recently abandoned California State Automobile Association headquarters in the heart of San Francisco. All of the men who had been hired to work as security guards at the building belonged to the BNG, meaning that bin Osman and his men would have the complete run of the place.

They had chosen the building because of its proximity to the hotels where the three traitorous Islamic leaders were staying. Those men suckled at the teat of Western decadence and were a disgrace to all of Islam, with their so-called progressive policies. They were moving their countries away from *Sharia* law and had to be eliminated. The fact that they would eliminate most of San Francisco, the most decadent city in the most decadent nation since the waning days of ancient Rome, was only icing on the cake.

Bin Osman had taken Maurstad with him to San Francisco, but first he had made the man watch as he carved up the scientist's wretched wife. The only thing that brought the scientist back to a state resembling sanity was the knowledge that if he didn't cooperate and arm the bomb, bin Osman would do the same to his daughter.

Not that bin Osman had any intention of sparing the girl. Botros knew that the main reason bin Osman kept the girl alive was because he intended to torture her, too, after the bomb was activated. After he had sliced the daughter into pieces in front of her father, Botros had no doubt that he would do the same to the father. Meaning that Botros and his men would have two more messes to clean up before they could leave this disgusting place.

A bleating car horn outside the door broke his train of thought. Botros looked through the viewing slot they'd built into the side of the building and saw that it was the BNG members who had been assigned to stalk Eddie Anderson. He knew they wouldn't be there if they hadn't killed or captured the young American. One of his men pressed a button on a box mounted on a steel post sunk into the cement to the left of the door, where it could be reached from the cab of a vehicle, and the big overhead door began to rise on its tracks toward the ceiling. A gaudy Mitsubishi with a racing wing drove into the building, followed by an equally gaudy pickup truck that rode just inches off the ground on ridiculously sized wheels and tires.

The BNG had no idea what Botros and bin Osman were up to; they'd been ordered to assist the men by their parent organization in the Philippines and like good soldiers they carried out their orders, but that didn't stop Botros from despising them as much as he despised all other Americans. The BNG members hadn't been informed of the plan to destroy San Francisco because the plan called for the BNG members to be destroyed with their city. These loyal soldiers in the service of decadence and depravity unknowingly worked to bring about their own demise, and they didn't appear to have the intelligence or intellectual curiosity to question what they were doing.

When they shut off their loud vehicles, Botros could hear the grating sound of Eddie Anderson's voice shouting curses at the Filipinos from the back seat of the car. It looked like the Filipinos wanted to beat the loudmouthed American into submission, but there didn't appear to be room in the cramped back seat to take a swing at him. Botros' suspicions were confirmed when the Filipinos dragged Anderson out of the car and began beating him.

Botros wished they had killed Anderson where they'd found him but he knew why they'd brought the American here. It was the same reason Botros couldn't let them beat the man to death in spite of the fact that doing so would be the most expedient route. He knew that the sick Malaysian who was calling the shots wanted the opportunity to torture Anderson, which was why they would be forced to keep the miserable creature alive until after bin Osman and his men returned from setting the bomb in San Francisco, which likely wouldn't be until early the next morning.

Botros worried that the Malaysian's twisted obsession would bring about the failure of their plan; every loose end was one more weak point in their plan, and the big American who had been tormenting them since Qatar was the loosest end of all. There should be no way for the man to know where they were or what they were doing, but he had already proved that he was capable of the impossible. He'd discovered the warehouse, and he'd uncovered Team Free Flow's link to the plutonium. He had almost discovered the plutonium twice, and he'd dispatched every team that Botros and bin Osman had sent after him with seeming ease.

Botros consoled himself with the fact that they should be safe here, and even if, by some miracle, Cooper did find his way to the compound, they'd placed well-armed guards around the perimeter of the building. Cooper's luck couldn't hold out forever.

THE HUMAN SCARECROW forced Bolan inside the trailer at gunpoint. If the man had ever possessed the capacity for abstract thought, the scrambling that his brains had taken from years of drug abuse had banished that capacity and he didn't bother to disarm the soldier, even though he wore his Desert Eagle on a leg holster outside of his pants and had the Fairbairn-Sykes strapped to the opposite leg. The man barely seemed to know where he was, but that didn't make the shotgun he pointed at the Executioner any less lethal.

The two entered the structure in what should have been a combination kitchen-living room, with the two spaces separated by a counter and overhead cupboards. But the kitchen had not seen any cooking in a long while, judging from the amount of trash piled on the stove and counters, and the living room had not seen any living, since it too was covered with garbage.

The place smelled like an indoor trash dump. The toothless man with the shotgun motioned for the Executioner to move down the hallway to the bedroom area where he'd seen the man injecting drugs earlier. Bolan checked each room they passed for signs of life, but saw none.

When they got to the bedroom, the smell changed from garbage to urine and sweat, but it wasn't the smell of normal sweat, the kind a person got from hard work; rather, it was the sick, salty smell of a junkie lying on a sidewalk in a pool of his own fluids. It was the smell of humans in the process of dying.

When they entered the room, the woman who had been unconscious earlier stirred and rose up. She made no attempt to cover her naked, emaciated body. "What you got there, Randy?" she asked.

"I found this one out poking around by the meth lab. He killed McVeigh."

It figures that this clown would name his dog after one

of America's most notorious terrorists, Bolan thought, but said nothing.

"I need you to go out and tell that Osman fellow that we caught some kind a soldier poking around the place."

"He left about an hour ago," the woman said. "They took that white van and headed north on the highway."

"Can you watch the big guy here, Lee Ann?" The man handed the shotgun to the woman.

Lee Ann gave a predatory look. "I think I can take care of him. Randy, you go on ahead and do what you have to do."

Bin Osman stood on the loading dock as the BNG member backed the white cargo van into the loading bay in the basement of the abandoned CSAA building. He followed it inside just before the BNG members who had been hired as security guards closed the overhead door behind them. He gave instructions and guided the forklift he'd rented as another gang member loaded the pallet that held the container with the plutonium. He had the driver transport it to the back of the loading area. Then he did the same with the explosive device that Maurstad had assembled. When bin Osman had the equipment where he wanted it, he went into the back of the van to get Maurstad himself.

He'd had the scientist bound tightly, but he probably needn't have worried; Maurstad lay on the floor in a nearly catatonic state, his soft weeping interrupted only by the occasional violent sob. Perhaps Botros had been correct; perhaps he had gone too far when he dismembered this man's wife before his very eyes. The act seemed to have destroyed the mind of his nuclear scientist, but as far as bin Osman was concerned, it had been worth the price.

He bent over the weeping man and grabbed him by the lapels of his sport jacket. "Dr. Maurstad," bin Osman said. "You must compose yourself. We still have work to do."

When he failed to get a response from the man he slapped him hard across the face. This caused the man to cast his wild eyes in bin Osman's direction. "You have seen the fate that is in store for your daughter if you do not cooperate, Dr. Maurstad. Now I suggest you pull yourself together and finish your work."

The mention of his daughter seemed to focus the man and after bin Osman untied him he stood, no longer sobbing, although on close inspection bin Osman noticed that tears still poured from his eyes.

"What do I do now?" he asked bin Osman.

"Now you arm the weapon with the plutonium and set the timer."

"I'll need an NBC suit."

"Of course you will." Bin Osman had one of his men get the Nuclear, Biological and Chemical protection suit they'd secreted away on the site. Bin Osman knew that Maurstad really didn't need an NBC suit—he would not live nearly long enough to develop cancer after handling the plutonium—but he couldn't tell Maurstad that if he wanted the man to cooperate and complete the final steps to activate the bomb.

Bin Osman would have to let the man and his daughter live long enough to ensure that the device Maurstad had assembled would work, which irritated him because his session with Mrs. Maurstad had whetted his appetite. He knew that normal people might consider his need to torture and kill sick; his college psychologist certainly had when she'd threatened to have him diagnosed as a psychopathic personality—but she hadn't lived long enough to carry out an official diagnosis. She had been bin Osman's last victim for nearly thirty years, until he'd signed on with Jemaah Islamiyah. Being part of the al Qaeda affiliate had afforded him ample opportunity to engage in his favorite pastime, and he was now making up for lost time.

Bin Osman helped Maurstad into the NBC suit and led him to the container, but once there, the scientist again became catatonic. Clearly he needed to be motivated. He needed what the Americans called a pep talk. "Dr. Maurstad," bin Osman said, "you really must compose yourself. You must think of your daughter."

"You bastard!" Maurstad shouted. "You touch my daughter and I'll kill you."

"Like you killed me when I touched your wife?" bin Osman asked. "I think not. You will sit there and watch me reduce her to nothing, one small slice at a time. And then she will be dead and it will be your turn. No, you cannot prevent this from happening by threatening me. You can only prevent this by completing your task."

"How can I be sure that you won't torture her even if I do finish this device?"

"You can't, but you must have complete faith that I will do to your daughter much worse than what I did to your wife if you do not complete the device or if it fails to go off."

"What if I make a mistake and the bomb is a dud?"

"For your daughter's sake, you had better hope that you make no such mistakes."

Bin Osman watched as Maurstad forced himself to begin the final assembly of the nuclear device. The man worked from diagrams that he'd sketched out earlier. Bin Osman had taken the opportunity to have his own explosive expert study the diagrams, and his expert had suggested some changes that would make it difficult for anyone to disable the device even if someone discovered it.

When Maurstad began the final assembly, the Malaysian said, "No, Dr. Maurstad, that is not how I want you to wire the timer. You must do as I say." Bin Osman instructed the scientist on how he wanted the wiring to be completed.

While Maurstad finished wiring the timer, bin Osman received a phone call. It was from Botros. "Musa, I have a present for you," Botros said.

"What is it, Jameed?"

"It's the young American. Shall I entertain him until you arrive, or should I have him leave immediately." Botros spoke cryptically in case someone was listening to the conversation, but he already knew the answer—bin Osman would want him to keep Anderson alive until he returned from San Francisco so he could torture the young rider. Botros wanted to dispose of him immediately, which is what any sane person would do.

As Botros had expected, bin Osman said, "Keep him entertained until I return." Bin Osman smiled inside his own NBC suit as he watched Maurstad complete the final assembly procedures on the timer, exactly as he had ordered him to do. While he would have to wait until after they had fled the country to practice his art on Maurstad's daughter, the Anderson boy would provide that night's entertainment.

BOLAN KNEW he had to act quickly to stop Randy from alerting the men in the turkey shed to his presence. The only way to do that would be to get Lee Ann close enough so that he could overpower her. It was clear the emaciated shell of a woman was barely able to form a clear thought. Bolan simply smiled at her. It worked. Instinctively she moved closer to him. He held out his left hand and she moved in toward him. As soon as she was close enough, he gave her jaw a sharp jab.

He'd tried to control his punch and just apply the minimum amount of force to knock her out, but the Executioner had no way of knowing the toll years of drug abuse had taken on her bones and he felt the woman's jaw collapse under his blow. She fell hard, hitting her head on the edge of the bed. She wasn't moving, but Bolan could see she was still breathing. Given her fragile state, he feared he might have seriously hurt the woman, but at that moment he couldn't worry about that—he had to try to rescue Eddie Anderson. Her drug abuse had turned her into the walking dead already.

The entire encounter with Lee Ann had taken less than half a minute so Randy couldn't have gotten very far. Bolan ran from the bedroom to try to intercept the addict. He looked out the filthy living room window and saw the scrawny drug fiend standing alongside a building that once must have been a pump house for a well. His back was turned toward the trailer. Judging from the position of his hands, he'd stopped to urinate.

Bolan took the sound-suppressed Beretta from the shoulder rig he wore beneath his blouse and crept to the trailer door. He slowly made his way toward the oblivious drug addict. As he approached, Randy turned and the Executioner struck him hard on the temple with the Beretta. Randy collapsed to the ground, his penis still in his hands.

Bolan went back to the building that housed the meth lab and retrieved the binoculars he'd dropped when the dog had attacked him. The dog's carcass had already started to attract flies. Bolan crouched in the tall weeds that covered the entire compound and put camouflage grease paint on his face. The sun was beginning to set and in the twilight he was just able to make out the men inside the derelict cars guarding the building. From his position he could see three corners of the building, and one car had been placed at each corner. There was likely at least one such guard placed behind the building, at the farthest corner from the Executioner's vantage point. Even with a suppressor, his Beretta still made a fairly loud crack, so he'd either have to try to snipe at the men from far enough away so that they couldn't hear the shots or else sneak up on them and take them out one at a time with his Fairbairn-Sykes knife.

The problem with trying to snipe at the men from a distance was that the subsonic rounds would lose velocity and fall off at longer distances, meaning he'd have to use a fair amount of Kentucky windage. But even if he did hit his mark his bullets might not have the velocity to take out his targets. It looked like he was going to have to do this the hard way, with his knife.

Bolan slowly crept toward the vehicle nearest him.

The sun had set by the time Bolan closed in on the junked Chevrolet Caprice placed at the corner of the turkey shed nearest the meth lab. The soldier had crawled on his belly through the tall weeds, taking his time to avoid upsetting the weeds and giving away his position. Now he waited near the edge of the road that ran through the property, looking for the best way across.

He didn't see one. Even with the sun now below the horizon, there was no way to cross the road without alerting the sentry in the car. He was within less than fifty yards from the man, within range of the powered-down subsonic ammo in his suppressed Beretta, but Bolan wanted to be sure. In the flat twilight it was often hard to judge distances accurately. He studied the distance, looked at a couple of objects in between him and the target for scale, and estimated the range to be a bit less than forty yards. He set the selector to single-round fire and sighted the man's face in the center of his night sights. He squeezed the trigger and even with the sound suppressor, the gun seemed to roar in his hand.

But his aim was true and a large crater appeared right at the bridge of the man's nose. His head snapped back in the seat and his sightless eyes stared up at the rotting roof of the car.

To Bolan the shot from the Beretta sounded like cannon fire, but he hoped the sound hadn't carried to the other sentries. He took out his binoculars and checked the other two sentries he could see from his position. The man at the far end of the shed on the side of the building that faced the road seemed oblivious to the shot, but the man at the near end on the opposite side of the building seemed to have heard something. He sat in a wrecked early 1970s Oldsmobile convertible and had a good view of the area from which Bolan had taken his shot. He had become alert and was looking around.

The man at the far end of the building was too far away for Bolan to get a shot off, but he estimated that the man in the convertible was still within sixty yards—a long shot with the powered-down ammo, but doable for someone as familiar with his equipment as the Executioner was. He'd taken longer shots with the 93-R and made them, even using subsonic ammo.

The man in the Oldsmobile couldn't see the sentry Bolan had just shot because of the position of the cars, but Bolan had a clear view of the man sitting in the front seat of the enormous convertible. When he saw the sentry raise a walkie-talkie to his lips, he quickly drew a bead on the man and squeezed the trigger. He aimed for the very top of the sentry's head but because of bullet drop, the round hit the man just between his nose and top lip. His head flipped back and the

Executioner put another round into the top of his throat, at the base of the skull. Bolan saw the top of the man's head explode in a spray of bone, hair and gray matter as the bullet exited, and then he fell backwards and out of sight.

The man at the far end of the building hadn't moved. Bolan scoped him out through his binoculars and saw that he was in the middle of enjoying a cigarette. He, too, sat in an Oldsmobile convertible, but in his case he sat in a smaller model. The top was up and remained relatively intact. Bolan could see that wires ran from buds in the sentry's ears down toward his lap, most likely to an MP3 player. They could have been connected to some sort of communications equipment, but judging from the way the man was bobbing his head, the soldier doubted that was the case.

Bolan crept in the tall weeds alongside the road. The building angled away from the road, so by the time he was parallel with the man, his target was more than sixty yards away from the soldier. Because of the angle, Bolan couldn't see if there were any more guards behind the building or at the corner, but he guessed there was at least one. He didn't want to chance alerting a sentry he couldn't see or stop before the man might alert others in the complex, but because the sentry in the car near him was rocking out, he had an opportunity to sneak across the road undetected.

Bolan watched the sentry singing along and noted that at regular intervals he threw his head back, closed his eyes and seemed to sing a repeated chorus. Bolan counted out the beats between these episodes and timed his dash across the road to coincide with the man throwing his head back. He ran low across the road and ducked behind an overturned wooden skiff with a hole in its side big enough for Bolan to crawl through. He ducked under the skiff and peered through the hole at the singing sentry. He had just finished his chorus and was opening his eyes. He'd seen nothing when Bolan ran across the road.

Tall weeds had grown up between the turkey shed and the road, giving Bolan cover as he crept toward the sentry. Because the convertible's top was up, there was a fairly large blind spot between the turkey shed and the car, which was placed so that it faced the road. The car looked almost drivable—the tires even still contained air and fake spoke hubcaps still covered the two wheels that Bolan could see. Best of all, the sideview mirrors were still intact. Bolan used the mirror on the passenger's side of the car to ascertain the location of the blind spot for the man singing away in the driver's seat. The soldier looked in the mirror and when he was in a position where he couldn't see the driver, he was almost certainly in a position where the driver couldn't see him. Using this method he got to the car's rear bumper.

Bolan crawled around to the driver's side of the car and made his way to the driver's door. The guard finally spotted him and reached for his weapon. Gripping his Fairbairn-Sykes in his right hand, Bolan lunged up and in one fluid motion grabbed the man's hair with his left hand, tilted back his head and cut his throat, slicing through the cords that ran from the ear buds.

Knowing the man was dead, the soldier dove back into the weeds and crept to the corner of the building. Looking through the weeds he saw one more car, another aging convertible, this one an old Pontiac LeMans from the mid 1960s. Another sentry sat in the car, this one alert and scanning his surroundings. By the time he saw the Executioner it was too late. Bolan drew a bead on the man with his Beretta and with one gentle squeeze of the smooth trigger, he sent a bullet right into the man's temple as he fumbled for his own gun.

Knowing that he'd need as much ammo as possible when things turned ugly, Bolan replaced the partially spent magazine with a full one and moved to the building to position himself for a look around the corner. He saw one more guard, this one standing by the door of what once must have been some sort of washing room or cleaning room built on the side of the main structure. He studied the surrounding area but couldn't see any more guards or any likely hides for them.

Off in the area that once must have been the turkey's pasture, Bolan could see a drainage ditch that ran alongside the fence and terminated very near the barn entrance. Bolan moved into the ditch, crouched and ran toward the small cleaning room. When he reached the point where the ditch became too shallow to crouch without being seen, he crawled on his belly until he reached the end of the trench. A small pipe ran into the trench from the room built onto the side of the barn.

The final guard was only four feet from where Bolan hid in the ditch. He waited patiently and when the man turned his back, the soldier lunged out and attacked him. He had the man in a death grip before he'd had a chance to make a sound. Bolan twisted the man's head hard. The man looked at Bolan with a calm expression on his face, then fell face-first onto the ground, dead. Bolan moved quickly toward the door that led into the small lean-to built onto the side of the turkey shed.

The structure had windows on the three sides that weren't connected to the shed, but they were so filthy it was impossible to see through them. Bolan crouched down below the windows in case it was easier to see out than in and moved to the door. When he craned his head to look inside, he saw something he hadn't expected. A young girl was chained to an old, dusty cast-iron sink. A man with an SAR-21 battle rifle stood above her, the short barrel of his rifle trained on her head.

Botros hated the fact that his men were being drawn into the culture of decadence that was motorcycle racing. They had begun listening to popular music, and he suspected that some of them had even begun smoking marijuana since they had been working with the deviant Filipino gangsters from San Francisco.

He watched the Filipino-American swine pummel Eddie Anderson on the floor of the shed. His men still hadn't cleaned up the bloody lump of carved flesh tied to the chair near where the gangsters beat the young American. He knew he should stop the beating—his life might be worth no more than Anderson's if he let these thugs accidentally killed the little man—but he found he was taking too much pleasure in the young man's suffering to stop the proceedings.

Ultimately the beating stopped on its own. As more of the gangsters noticed the grotesquery tied to the chair, they lost interest in beating Anderson. Eventually they stopped altogether. The sight of Nancy Maurstad's remains even quieted the abrasive young American. It was the first time Botros had ever seen the man when he wasn't flapping his lips about something.

"Tie him up," Botros ordered the Filipinos, motioning to a chair not far from bin Osman's previous victim.

By this time the shock had worn off and Anderson resumed

his tirade against both Botros and the Filipinos. The Filipinos began to punch the man again.

"Stop. We must keep him alive. Gag him with this." Botros tossed a filthy rag to the Filipino closest to him and the man stuffed the rag in Anderson's mouth, then secured it with a piece of duct tape.

Bin Osman had been pleased when Botros had called to tell him about the abduction of the American. Botros loathed the Malaysian, but it comforted him when his psychopathic boss was pleased. He looked at the hideous carcass tied to the chair in the middle of the room. It had been several hours since she'd died and most of the blood had drained from her body, leaving her looking like a beached manatee. While he thought bin Osman's actions were despicable, he was glad that the Malaysian was going to practice his art on Anderson rather than him.

He was further relieved that the big American had not found them yet. Perhaps he would never find them. Botros didn't know who he feared more—bin Osman or Cooper. Even though the depths of bin Osman's depravity knew no bottom, he thought perhaps he feared Cooper more. Bin Osman was a man—a twisted, emotionally stunted excuse of a man, but still a man. He wasn't so sure about Cooper. He had begun to believe that the American really was *Iblis* made flesh.

But the more time passed without their being attacked by the big American, the more relaxed Botros became. The plan would succeed; it had to. The Muslim world needed to be rid of the traitorous bastards who spoon-fed their people Western decadence disguised as moderation.

They would strike what may well turn out to be a death blow to the United States. By destroying a major U.S. city like San Francisco, the United States would likely become a police state, as it nearly had after the glorious attacks of 9/11. The Americans were so cowardly that after one attack on their own soil they had gladly handed over their freedoms to the government. Their president at the time had claimed that the attackers hated America because of its freedom; in reality, Botros thought, they had hated America for its presence in the Middle East and its support of Israel. Its citizens' so-called "freedom" was just an aspect of what they hated, a symptom of the disease just as a sneeze was a symptom of a cold.

Botros knew al Qaeda did want the American government to curtail the freedom of its citizens, not because they hated that freedom but because the discontent such action would create would in turn create much internal strife that al Qaeda could manipulate to achieve its own ends. They had almost accomplished this after 9/11, but as time went on without further attacks, the American people had slowly begun to reclaim their freedoms.

The bomb that bin Osman was in the process of activating would kill nearly all of the people in San Francisco, and it would kill hundreds of thousands in the surrounding area. The fallout from the bomb would kill hundreds of thousands more. After the attack the government would almost certainly declare martial law. The chaos that would result from this would throw the United States into such a state of turmoil that controlling the chaos would consume all of the country's resources. It would force the U.S. to withdraw much of its military forces from around the world. This would leave al Qaeda free to achieve its aims without American interference.

It would work. Botros could feel it in his bones. By this time, Maurstad should have finished assembling the bomb and set the timer. The bomb would be set to go off at 6:00 p.m.

the following evening, in almost exactly twenty-four hours. By that time everyone would have returned from the races and the Egyptian, the Saudi, and the Jordanian traitors would be back in the city. Bin Osman should be returning to the compound within half an hour. After that, it would just be a matter of waiting. Waiting, and watching for that devil Cooper.

Botros knew he had to stop worrying about the American. Everything was going as planned.

THE MAN GUARDING the young woman hadn't noticed the Executioner peering through the doorway, which was partially open to let air flow into the hot room. The guard was too busy staring at the girl's thighs, which were uncovered because her skirt had ridden up on her hip, exposing a lacy pale pink undergarment. The guard seemed transfixed by the sight, as if he'd never seen a woman before. Bolan watched as the man moved closer to the girl.

Just then the girl saw Bolan's face through the doorway. Her eyes went wide, but Bolan held a finger to his lips, indicating she should remain quiet. The fact that she didn't scream even when she saw the soldier's grease-painted face in the doorway told him that she was either nearly catatonic or else very tough.

The girl looked at the guard and spread her legs, moving the skirt even farther up her hip. Then she gave the guard a seductive smile.

The guard glanced through the door into the main area of the shed to make certain no one could see him, then moved closer to the girl. Bolan crept closer to the doorway and prepared to move. The guard reached down to touch the girl's leg. It looked to Bolan as if the man was shaking. When he reached down to unbuckle his pants, Bolan made his move. He leaped through the door with the Fairbairn-Sykes knife in an ice pick grip and drove it down into the man's sterno-clavicular junction. The blade sliced through the man's jugular vein and he collapsed before he even knew he'd been attacked.

Again Bolan held his finger up to his lip, indicating that the girl should remain quiet, and glanced out the door into the main area of the shed. In the middle of the room he could see what most likely had been a female human, though she'd been sliced into such a gory mess that the soldier couldn't be completely certain. Her bloodless body was tied to a chair. Next to her Eddie Anderson was tied to a similar chair, his face bloodied and bruised.

A more thorough survey of the room revealed several vehicles, including the two he'd followed to the compound after Anderson had been kidnapped. He saw about a dozen Arab-looking men, who must have been Botros men, along with six Filipinos.

The soldier had faced some impossible odds in his life and come out on top—odds a lot worse than eighteen to one—but his luck had to run out sometime. Just because he'd faced worse didn't mean eighteen to one odds were good. He had to play this smart or he'd not only get himself killed, but he'd also bring about the deaths of Anderson and the girl, whom he assumed was Mareebeth Maurstad. He wished he'd have called in Osborne, but he'd been too busy trying to rescue Anderson to take the time to call for help.

Bolan needed some sort of diversion. He was still trying to figure out what form that diversion might take when he heard a cell phone ring. He watched as Jameed Botros pulled a phone from his pants pocket and said, "Did it go well?"

Botros appeared pleased with the answer. "How far out are you?" he asked. When he apparently got the answer he hung up his phone. "Open the door," he ordered. "They are coming up the road."

MUSA BIN OSMAN hoped the Filipinos in the truck with him would not notice that he was excited. His heart pounded when he thought about the task before him, and he plotted out every cut he planned to make on the American's body before he finally released him into death. He probably wouldn't take as much time as he had with the Maurstad woman, but the youngster had caused him problems and for that he would pay.

When the van drove up to the overhead door that he'd had installed in the turkey shed, he looked at the guards Botros had placed in the derelict cars around the building. In one car he could see no one and in the other the sentry appeared to be asleep. Botros would pay for the incompetence of his men. By the time the door had been raised and the Filipino driving had shut off the engine of the van, he'd worked himself into a complete state of rage.

"You incompetent fool!" he shrieked at Botros.

"What is the problem?" Botros asked.

"It's the men you have guarding the building," bin Osman shouted. "They are either asleep or they have left their posts."

"That is impossible. They are good men, and experienced. They would never fail me."

"If it is impossible, what has happened to them? I clearly saw one man sleeping in the vehicle near the door, and his counterpart seems to have disappeared entirely," bin Osman shouted.

"Hadad!" Botros addressed one of his men. "Go and see

if this is true. If these men are indeed absent or sleeping, find them and bring them in here."

Hadad ran from the building to go and check on the guards.

"If what you say is true," Botros said to bin Osman, "I will see to it that the men are punished."

"You will if you do not want to be punished yourself," bin Osman warned.

"Did you run into any problems arming the device?" Botros asked. They had been able to speak freely around the BNG members because none of them spoke Arabic. Most spoke only English with only a smattering of Tagalog because they had been in San Francisco since they were small children.

"Only a bit of reluctance on the part of Dr. Maurstad," bin Osman said. "Bring Dr. Maurstad out here," he ordered in English.

One of the Filipinos opened the rear door of the van's cargo box and two more BNG members emerged with Gunthar Maurstad sandwiched between them. When the man saw the remains of his wife tied to the chair, he almost collapsed, but the Filipinos on either side of him held him upright.

"When I reminded him that his cooperation was the only possible way to spare his daughter the same fate his wife met, he became much more helpful."

Once the device exploded, Botros knew his deviant master would deconstruct the younger Maurstad woman with at least as much care as he'd dismembered her mother.

In the meantime, bin Osman could work on the young racer. And Botros would have two more people to guard for the next twenty-four hours. It seemed bin Osman did not care how much extra work he made for Botros and his men. As he contemplated the disrespect that bin Osman seemed to have for him, Botros heard three loud popping sounds from behind him, as if someone had set off three small firecrackers. He turned to look for the source of the sound, but was interrupted by a distraught Hadad, who came rushing into the building at that very instant.

"They're dead!" Hadad shouted.

"Who's dead," Botros asked.

"All of them," the shocked man said.

"All of who?" Botros asked, getting impatient with the man's circular discourse.

"The guards. All of them, dead."

Botros heard four more of the popping sounds in rapid succession and Hadad fell flat on his face, a large chunk missing from the back of his head.

14

When Botros sent the man he called Hadad to go check on the sentries, Bolan still hadn't formulated a good plan but he knew his time for formulating had run out. It was time to act. From his hide behind a crate that had likely housed components for the nuclear explosive device that bin Osman and Botros had assembled, he counted the men in the room, noted their locations and decided the order in which he planned to shoot them. If he was really fast and his timing perfect, he'd be able to cut the odds against him in half before anyone had a chance to fire back.

Unfortunately those odds had gotten much worse since the van full of more BNG members arrived. In addition to bin Osman, six Filipinos had exited the van, meaning the soldier was now facing twenty-five-to-one odds.

The three men closest to him had bunched up fairly close together. Two sat on an old bus seat smoking cigarettes and another sat on a chair right beside them. He could take out all three in a fraction of a second. Next he would aim for the men standing in the center of the room, where most of the Filipinos had gathered. Then he'd shoot at the men on the other side of the van. He figured he could take out twelve or thirteen men before they even realized they were under attack, but only if his timing was perfect.

The Executioner knew it was time to act when he saw the walk-in door beside the overhead door open. It could only be Hadad coming back to report that he'd killed the sentries. As soon as he saw the doorknob start to turn, he fired at the three men closest to him. Several of the men farther away heard the popping of his Beretta and turned to see what had happened. At that moment Hadad burst through the door and began shouting about all the sentries being dead.

Bolan took the opportunity to draw a bead on one of the Filipinos standing in the center of the room, near the cargo van, and in quick succession he shot down three of the gang-bangers, along with Hadad, whose head the soldier blew apart in midsentence. At that point everyone left standing ran for cover, drawing their weapons as they ran, but the Executioner was able to pick off four more of them before they'd found a decent hiding spot.

In the confusion no one seemed to have located his hide and several men hadn't chosen locations that provided cover from him. He saw the spiked hair of one of the BNG members poking up from behind a wooden work bench. Just enough of the skull showed to make it worth taking a shot. Bolan aimed just millimeters above the top of the workbench and squeezed the trigger. The man's scalp flew off the top of his head, spiked hairdo and all, along with a four-inch section of his skull and a fair-sized chunk of his brain.

Another man had found a better hiding spot, but his left arm protruded from the corner of the cardboard box that he hid behind. Using the man's arm as a starting point, Bolan estimated where the man's center of mass was and fired three rounds into that area. His estimate must have been sound, because the arm dropped to the ground and didn't move.

The slide of his Beretta locked open and Bolan reached for another magazine. The time for stealth was over so the soldier replaced the empty magazine with one loaded with high-power ammunition. Then he removed the Desert Eagle from his leg holster. He had to find a new spot soon or they'd figure out where he was and blow him to pieces right through the wooden crate. He set the selector on the Beretta to tri-burst and blasted suppression fire with both guns as he dove for the rear bumper of a Toyota Tacoma parked along the wall to his left.

The remaining men opened up at the area where they'd just seen him, but Bolan moved around to the front of the truck where the engine block would provide better cover than the sheet metal bodywork. He reloaded his handguns on the fly, and lay down on the ground behind the front wheel. He looked around the tire and saw the lower torsos of two men crouched behind the white cargo van, firing toward the rear of the Tacoma. With two quick shots Bolan put a .44 Magnum round from his Desert Eagle into the groins of each man, shattering their pelvises and most likely ensuring that if they did live, they would not sire any children. Both men fell behind the van where Bolan couldn't see them.

His shots attracted the attention of the BNG members who had taken cover near the door and they began firing at his position with their SAR-21s. The air around him filled with flying 5.56 mm bullets, ricocheting around the truck. Sooner or later a stray round was going to hit him. Bolan estimated that there were six to eight men in the area, but what really interested him was the object behind which one of the men hid—the oxygen and acetylene tanks of an acetylene torch. Bolan pulled the pin on a fragmentation grenade, counted to three and lobbed it at the tanks.

Even though he was behind the Toyota pickup, Bolan felt the fireball roll over him, singing his hair and eyebrows. The men in that corner of the room fared much worse. The man behind the tank had virtually disappeared, leaving nothing behind but a grease spot on the cement floor, and the two men nearest him lay on the ground bleeding out from great rifts in their torsos and limbs that were missing completely.

Three men had caught fire and ran around like human matchsticks. Three other men seemed to have escaped harm from the explosion, but they ran out to the middle of the room, right into Bolan's field of fire. Three quick shots from the Desert Eagle put them down, and another three ended the suffering of the flaming men.

As quickly as the firefight had started, it ended. Bolan checked all corners of the room, but it was empty, except for Anderson, who remained tied up in the center of the room. The fireball had singed his hair and burned his eyebrows off, but he seemed relatively unscathed. Otherwise all that remained were dead Saudis and Filipinos. He saw no sign of Botros or bin Osman. Nor did he see any sign of Maurstad. He'd been counting on rescuing Maurstad so he could find out where the bomb was located and learn how to disarm it.

Bolan heard an engine start up outside and a vehicle roar away.

He had to catch the men and rescue Maurstad, but he couldn't leave Anderson and the Maurstad girl tied up in a burning barn. He cut the ropes holding Anderson, tore off his duct-tape gag and asked the young man, "Are you all right?"

"I'm fine. I have to get that cocksucker."

"You mean Botros?"

"Yeah, I know he killed my brother." Anderson ran to the

low-rider pickup and started to pull his bike out of the box. "Help me get this out," he said, "and I'll follow them to see where they go."

Bolan went to help the young racer. "I'll help you on one condition," he said.

"What condition?"

"When they get wherever they're going, you call me before you go after them."

"Fuck that," Anderson said.

"I mean it. You want to get these guys, right?"

"Damned right I do."

"Then we'll get them together. Alone you don't stand a chance."

"How will I call you?" Bolan gave him his cell phone number. "Where will you be?" Anderson asked.

"I'll be as close behind you as possible," Bolan said. "But first I have to take care of someone."

Anderson checked over his bike to make sure it was road-worthy after the crash, grabbed his helmet from inside the Mitsubishi and tore out of the building through the walk-in door, which was still open.

MAREEBETH Maurstad heard the gunshots from the main building. Then she heard the explosion and now she could hear the sound of a raging fire. She'd been trying to break through her bonds for nearly two days with no luck, but she continued to work them. Then a large shadow appeared in the doorway. This is it, she thought. This is when I'm going to die.

The large man approached her with a long knife in his hands and bent over her. He sliced the knife downward and she held her breath, waiting for it to sink into her flesh. But instead of cutting her, it cut the ropes holding her feet. Then it cut the ropes holding her hands.

It was the tall soldier who had killed the man she thought was going to rape her.

"Are you all right?" he asked.

"I think so. What about my father?"

"I think he's all right," the man said, "but he's been taken away with the men who had you kidnapped."

"What about my mother?" The man remained silent. "Is she all right?"

"She's dead," the man replied.

The girl felt the wind rush from her lungs, as if she'd just been punched in the gut. The big man was already talking on his cell phone, telling someone named Bear to get a helicopter here as soon as possible. While he spoke, she tried to run into the burning barn to see her mother, but the big man stopped her before she could get through.

He hung up the phone and said, "You can't go in there. We have to get out of here before this whole place goes up in flames." He led the girl out of the building and they jogged along the road away from the buildings while the flames grew higher and higher behind them. After they'd gone a ways the man walked off the road and pulled some brush aside, revealing a motorcycle. He rolled it out on the road and turned on the ignition key. When he turned the key, the motorcycle's lights came on.

The man looked up at the sky and the girl saw a helicopter flying in from over the hills to the east. It landed on the road in front of the motorcycle. The big soldier put his hand on the girl's shoulder and ushered her toward the helicopter. When he helped her climb inside, she marveled at the gentleness of his touch. She had witnessed these hands take a human life with more ease than most people display opening a jar of peanut butter, yet when they lifted her up into the helicopter they displayed a tenderness completely at odds with their rough texture.

What the girl didn't know was that the act of killing can engender a respect for the sanctity of life. The Executioner put more effort into saving lives than taking them. When he had to kill, he only did so to protect innocents like her.

"You'll save my daddy, right?" the girl asked.

"I'll try my best," the soldier said. He wished he could be more positive, but he couldn't lie to her; her father was in terrible danger and there were no guarantees. Then the helicopter rose into the air and the big man and his motorcycle faded into the night.

AFTER THE HELICOPTER LEFT, Bolan stripped out of his fatigues and put on his blacksuit. He topped off his magazines and put his weapons into their respective holsters and sheaths, then put on his riding suit over his gear. He was just about to put on his helmet when the phone vibrated in his vest pocket.

It was Anderson. "They've gone to their garages at the track," he said.

"Sit tight," Bolan told him. "I'll be there in half an hour."

Traffic was almost nonexistent and Bolan rode the bike harder than he had ever ridden a motorcycle on public streets, slowing only to ride through populated areas. He averaged over a hundred miles an hour and arrived at Laguna Seca in a little over twenty minutes. He found Anderson near the garage area twenty-five minutes after he'd put away his cell phone.

"There's a bunch of them in there," Anderson said when

Bolan parked his bike. "I've counted at least six guys going into the garages and none of them have come back out. What are we going to do?"

Bolan surveyed the situation. Even though it was the middle of the night, the entire place was alive with activity—motorcycle engines revved in garages, people came and went, delivering parts and other supplies, air wrenches spun away, various tools banged and clanged away. It was the night before the big race and motorcycles were being rebuilt, their engines overhauled, their wheels being covered with new race rubber. This activity would continue through the night right up until the next afternoon's race.

"Is there a back way into the garage complex?" Bolan asked.

"Yeah, there are back doors to all the garages. It's a long way around to the back, but we can take a shortcut through the Ducati garages. Follow me."

Bolan and Anderson jogged over to the Ducati garage complex and went inside.

"Where've you been all day?" a man asked Anderson. "And what happened to your eyebrows?"

"Let's talk later," Anderson said. "I've got to do something."

"You've got to get your ass to bed," the man said. "What the hell? Are you on drugs or something?"

"Look, man," Anderson said, "you're my manager and I love you like a brother, but you have to believe me—this is important. Have I ever lied to you or let you down before?"

"Never."

"I'm not my brother. I know he broke your heart when you managed him, but I'm not him. Please believe me when I tell you that this is a matter of life or death."

"Who's your friend?" the manager asked. "You know you're not supposed to let anyone in here the night before a race."

"It's important," Anderson reiterated. "You're just going to have to trust me."

Anderson and Bolan jogged out the back of the Ducati garage complex and broke into a run until they reached the Free Flow complex. The door was locked.

"Stand back," Bolan said. He pulled a gun with a sound suppressor screwed to the end and fired into the lock. Anderson was surprised at how loud the gun was—in the movies they just coughed a bit. Still, there was so much background noise around the garage area that no one would have noticed the shot.

"Stay here," Bolan told Anderson just before he kicked open the door. While the door swung open he lurched to the side in case someone took a shot at them. When no bullets flew through the door he glanced around the corner. The area immediately behind the door was empty and unlit, but Bolan could see lights on in the area where Botros had set up his office.

The Executioner checked to make sure that Anderson wasn't following him and entered the building. A couple of men appeared in the doorway separating the storage area in the back of the garage from the main part of the complex. Bolan ducked behind some boxes and watched them head back to the door. The first man looked at the destroyed lock and said something to his partner in Arabic, but before the man had a chance to process his partner's words, Bolan fired a round into the back of his head. The man who'd examined the door reached for a gun but his hand hadn't yet touched the grip sticking out of the waistband of his pants before the Executioner punched a round through his forehead.

Bolan spun toward a noise he heard coming from the doorway and fired at a figure that had appeared, dropping the man to the ground. He moved along the wall until he reached the doorway and glanced around the corner. Before he could see anything a hand grabbed his neck and spun him around through the door, right into a roundhouse punch that would have dropped him, had the hand around his neck not been holding him up. Two other men came into what was suddenly a very fuzzy picture for the soldier. Each man grabbed an arm and slammed Bolan up against the doorframe. The man who had hit the soldier began to pummel him.

Bolan saw a silver streak come down from his right and the man who was hitting him dropped to the ground. Though he wasn't quite sure what had just happened, his instincts took over and he brought both of his shoulders back against the Adam's apples of the men trying to hold his arms still. It wasn't enough to take the men out of action, but once again Bolan saw the silver streak come down across the head of the man on his right. This time Bolan had regained his wits enough to see that it was Eddie Anderson swinging a large torque wrench. Both the man who had been punching him and the man who had been holding his right arm lay on the ground, their brains exposed through large gashes in their skull.

Bolan swung his right arm around and punched his knuckles into the throat of the man still holding his left arm. He felt the trachea collapse beneath his knuckles, but he held the man up and gave him another powerful punch in the throat, just to be certain. The man collapsed to the ground, choking to death.

15

When the bullets started flying, bin Osman grabbed Maurstad and ran for the door with Botros hot on his heels. He watched through the open door as the American devil mowed down man after man. Botros had been correct; this man was *Iblis* made flesh. Bin Osman threw Maurstad into the back seat of a BMW sedan and shouted at Botros to drive.

They had barely made it out into the driveway when something inside the shed exploded. Botros looked at the building in his rearview mirror and saw flames melting the corrugated metal walls by the overhead doors. He got out to Highway One and pushed the German sports sedan to its absolute limits, taking the curves of the Coastal Highway as fast as the sophisticated combination of German suspension and Japanese tires would allow. Even though the BMW has one of the best-engineered suspensions available, it threatened to let go and the tires howled in protest, but Botros kept the car just within its limit and they made it back to Laguna Seca without crashing.

Maurstad had finally lost his mind completely. Bin Osman couldn't tell if he was laughing or crying, but he was pretty sure Maurstad didn't know himself. When bin Osman started to worry that he might go as mad as Maurstad if he had to keep listening to Maurstad's caterwauling, he punched the man in the jaw and knocked him unconscious. Maurstad still hadn't woken up when they pulled into Laguna Seca. The security guard gave bin Osman and Maurstad a suspicious look, but bin Osman just said, "The infidel has had too much to drink." Bin Osman laughed at his joke, as did Botros, but the guard just gave them a forced smile.

Once inside the garage complex, the pair carried the still-unconscious Maurstad to the office area and had their men stand guard against the attack they knew was coming.

"He's *Iblis,* I tell you," Botros said. "He's come to take us to Hell."

"You idiot," bin Osman said. "There is no *Iblis.* He is a man who just happens to be very good at what he does."

"You blaspheme!" Botros yelled. "There is an *Iblis* as sure as there is a Heaven and a Hell."

"You fool. We can never hope to understand Heaven and Hell. Simply thinking of them as concrete places is the real blasphemy."

Botros had finally had enough of his so-called superior. Bin Osman had served his purpose. He'd obtained the plutonium and the technical expertise to build the bomb, and he'd built the network that allowed them to plant the bomb and activate it in the heart of San Francisco. For all this Botros was grateful.

But to achieve all that Botros had been forced to allow a deviant to practice his perverted hobby on countless people over the past couple of years. It compromised Botros and worse yet, it compromised the plan. Every time Botros had been forced to leave someone alive so that bin Osman could torture them later, he had been putting himself, his people and the plan in jeopardy.

Botros had had enough. The Malaysian fancied himself the leader of this operation, and as long as he controlled essential aspects of the plan, Botros had been content to let him believe this, but now this weakling had become a liability. Botros had no doubt that if the big American devil captured him, bin Osman would roll over and give up the plan. He would tell the man where he could find the bomb, how to disarm it and probably the names of everyone who had worked on the plan from its inception. He was as weak as the now-conscious American lying in a heap on the floor, whimpering like a young schoolgirl.

And now this deviant who had been polluted by Western decadence was lecturing Botros about blaspheming? That was more than Botros could tolerate. Before the swine could open his mouth again, Botros drew his dagger and in one hard swipe, he sliced the man's neck open, nearly cutting off his head. Blood sprayed the entire office area, covering both Botros and Maurstad.

Before Botros had a chance to clean the blood off his face, arms, and chest, he heard commotion in the storage area at the back of the garage complex. He heard the muffled pops that he'd learned to recognize as the American devil's suppressed handgun, and he heard thuds that sounded like fists hitting flesh. Then all went quiet.

Botros held no illusions that his men had finally beaten Cooper. He didn't care. As long as the American didn't capture him or Maurstad, he had no way of finding the nuclear device and no way of stopping the plan from working. He lifted up the blood-soaked scientist and placed his Glock handgun to the man's head.

When Botros saw the large form appear in the doorway, he knew it could only be Cooper coming for him. The little spider monkey in his wake could only be Anderson. Botros thrust Maurstad in front of him and waited for the two Americans to enter the room. When the big devil saw him, he froze.

"Welcome, Mr. Cooper," Botros said.

BOLAN AND ANDERSON MOVED SLOWLY into the main part of the garage area, Bolan's Beretta leading the way. A flash of movement from the office area caught the Executioner's attention. He turned to see two figures bathed in fresh blood emerge from the makeshift office. At first he couldn't tell who they were, but upon closer study he realized it was Botros and Maurstad. He looked behind the two men and saw bin Osman crumpled to the floor, his head dangling from his neck. Botros held a gun to Maurstad's head and used the nuclear scientist as a human shield.

"Welcome, Mr. Cooper," Botros said.

The Executioner leveled the gun at the pair. He'd assessed the situation and deduced Botros' plan right off—kill everyone who could give up the location of the bomb, including himself. The overweight scientist made a complete shield for the smaller Saudi. Bolan couldn't get a clean kill shot at him, and that's what it had to be. Botros not only had his finger on the Glock's trigger, but he'd squeezed the trigger to the end of the cocking portion of its trigger stroke. The slightest pressure would send a bullet into Maurstad's brain, and Bolan needed the man alive if he had any hope of finding and disarming the nuclear bomb set to destroy the San Francisco area.

"Drop the gun," Bolan ordered, knowing full well that Botros would not comply. He was buying time, trying to line up a kill shot at Botros.

"Why would I do something so foolish?" Botros asked.

"To live." Again, Bolan knew that living would not tempt a fanatic like Botros, but he just wanted to keep the man talking.

"Live! Soon I will begin to live. Soon I will go to Heaven with the martyrs and will live in Paradise, away from you decadent infidels."

Bolan could see the muscles in the man's hand tense as he prepared to pull the trigger.

"Wait!" he shouted, not knowing what he'd say next, but relieved to see the muscles in the hand relax. "There must be something you want. A helicopter out of here, a fueled jet waiting for you at the airport. Something."

"I know what you want," Botros said. "You want this man so he can betray our plans and help you find the device he so kindly built in order to destroy his fellow Americans."

"We can work this out," Bolan said, trying to line up a good shot at Botros.

"Work *this* out," Botros said and squeezed the trigger of the Glock. The bullet entered Maurstad's face and flew out the opposite side of his head, taking most of the scientist's brain with it. Still holding up the lifeless carcass as a shield, Botros said, "Now you'll never find the bomb." He placed the barrel of the gun in his own mouth and pulled the trigger the final time.

Bolan looked at the two bodies crumpled on the floor before him. Mareebeth Maurstad was an orphan. His heart went out to the girl, but he knew she was tough—he'd seen it in her eyes when he rescued her. He hoped she'd be all right.

He'd failed. He'd just lost his last best hope for finding and disarming the nuclear bomb. If he was unable to do so, he'd have to have the president order an evacuation of the city, something that would cause almost as much chaos and social discord as a nuclear explosion. Given the short notice, tens of thousands of people would still likely die, and America would lose one of its most important cities. He'd have Hal Brognola get the president to start working up plans for an immediate evacuation, but the soldier still hoped it wouldn't come to that. He planned to do everything in his power to find and disarm the bomb.

That meant searching the Free Flow garages on the off chance that they might find some useful information. He was about to have Anderson help him with his search when he realized that the young man was on the verge of becoming unglued.

"You all right?" the soldier asked.

"I was going to kill him," Anderson said, looking down at Botros' lifeless body. "He killed my brother, and I was going to kill him."

"Well, he's dead now. You can want to kill him for the rest of your life and it won't change that fact. Dead is dead, and you can't undo that. Believe me, I wish I could."

The young man looked up at Bolan and said, "You don't understand."

"You think you are the only person who ever lost a loved one?" Bolan said. Anderson just looked at the man he knew as Matt Cooper and remained silent. "You think you are the only person who ever lusted for revenge? You think having this man die by your hand would somehow make what happened to your brother all right?

"Listen to me, kid. It doesn't make anything all right. It doesn't change a thing. Dead is still dead. This man was evil. He is gone and the world will be a better place for it. It doesn't matter how he died—he's dead.

"But right now I still have work to do or many more people

will die. I need to search this place for possible clues and I could use your help. Can you compose yourself and help me?"

"What do you want me to do?"

"Look for something, anything you can find that might have local addresses or lists of names, any information like that. They've planted a nuclear bomb and I have to find it."

Bolan began by searching the bodies. He found nothing of use on either bin Osman or Botros, but he hit the jackpot when examining Maurstad's body. In the vest pocket of his sport jacket the soldier found the detailed schematics and sketches, all hand-drawn, that appeared to have been the man's blueprints for assembling the bomb. That meant that he also had the instructions for disassembling it. He'd send them to Kurtzman right away and with some luck he'd find someone to interpret the schematics and get back to him with the exact instructions he'd need to neutralize the device before it went off.

But first he had to find it.

The Executioner used the downtime while he waited for Kurtzman to get back to him for a much-needed nap. He'd convinced Anderson to do the same. Anderson wanted to keep working with the soldier, but after much arguing Bolan had finally convinced him that he could best honor his brother by getting some rest and then going out and winning the race later in the day.

If there was a race to win.

If Bolan wasn't able to locate the bomb, the entire region was going to shut down and be thrown into a state of complete chaos. At that moment it was looking as if none of it mattered anymore anyway. Brognola and the president had concluded that evacuating the entire region was impossible. Tens of thousands, if not hundreds of thousands of people would be left behind, and thousands more would be killed in the ensuing panic.

The Executioner had no options. He had to succeed in this mission. The results of his failing were too terrible to allow. At least he would know how to dismantle the bomb should he be lucky enough to find it. He'd faxed Maurstad's notes to Kurtzman, who'd gotten them to some of the nation's top explosive experts. Kurtzman expected to have detailed instructions on dismantling the device to the soldier within the hour.

As for finding it, the loss of Maurstad, along with the deaths of Botros and his crew, bin Osman and all the Filipino gang-bangers working for him had eliminated almost all of the soldier's sources of information. In a last-ditch effort, he and Delbert Osborne planned to raid known BNG hangouts and try to find a gang member who knew where the bomb was. While the scientists studied Maurstad's schematics, Kurtzman worked his digital magic to find out where those hangouts were.

The problem was that these people almost certainly did not know anything about the bomb. Members of the BNG would be no more motivated to blow up their city and kill all of their families and friends than would any other San Francisco native, so Bolan was going to focus on finding someone left alive who had worked directly for bin Osman. The Executioner had thinned their ranks down to almost nothing since he'd arrived in Monterey, but he hoped there were at least a few gang members alive who knew where bin Osman had been working. They were his last chance, if they even existed.

Osborne was standing by waiting for the Executioner to call once Kurtzman got back to him with the locations of the hangouts. Osborne had provided some suspected locations to get Kurtzman started.

Bolan hadn't been asleep for forty-five minutes when the phone rang.

"What do you have for me, Bear?" Bolan said into his cell phone.

"Plenty, like how to dismantle an atomic bomb. Got a pen?"

"Yep, go ahead." Kurtzman read off the detailed instructions for dismantling the device described in Maurstad's schematics, complete with advice on what not to do if he wanted to avoid accidentally detonating the device. Bolan could have remembered the procedure without writing it down, but given the consequences of his failing, he took the most detailed notes he'd ever written. When he was through, he asked, "Got any info on known BNG hangouts?"

"That gets a little tricky," Kurtzman said. "These people aren't as organized as the Mafia or the Asian triads, but they do have one property that serves as something of a clubhouse. It's the top floor of a two-story building in Chinatown, on Grant Avenue between Pacific Avenue and Broadway, just south of Jack Kerouac Alley."

"What's on the bottom floor?" Bolan asked.

"A small Asian convenience store. The owner has strong ties with the BNG in the Philippines. The owner's cousin in the Philippines is under investigation for his ties to Jemaah Islamiyah, and he's also a major player in the BNG's Philippines operation. I'd say this is as good a place as any to start, Striker."

"I'd say you're right, but if I don't find something do you have any other locations to check out?"

"I'll find something," Kurtzman said.

Bolan called Osborne as soon as he hung up and gave him the Grant Street address.

"That makes sense," Osborne said. "That would have been the first place I looked. The cops have been watching that place for months."

"Where should we meet?" Bolan asked.

"There's a fish market across the street that opens early. How long until you can be there?"

"I'll meet you there in one hour," the Executioner replied.

BOLAN RODE UP THE HIGHWAY toward Castroville. The sun was barely poking up over the horizon, but the road leading from San Francisco to Monterey was a parking lot. Fortunately Bolan had the northbound lanes mostly to himself. Traffic was light and he zipped around cars and trucks easily. Then he noticed that he was being followed.

It didn't make much sense that someone would be following him—the men paying the bills for such an activity were both dead. If it was one of the BNG crews following him, they must have been at it for several days, and they couldn't yet know that bin Osman and Botros were dead. If that was the case, then why hadn't they been following him before?

The answer hit him—because he'd changed motorcycles. They were probably looking for the big BMW and had just figured out that he'd switched to the smaller one. That was the only thing that made sense. The reason they'd betrayed their presence was probably because he'd cranked up his pace after hitting Gilroy and they thought he was trying to get away.

Bolan saw what they were driving and knew he was in trouble. His followers were in a brand-new Nissan Skyline GT-R, one of the highest performing cars ever built, and much faster than the motorcycle Bolan rode. He had no chance of outrunning them, so he'd have to come up with another course of action.

As if his pursuers had read his mind, the driver of the Nissan supercar stomped on the accelerator and the car closed the distance between him and Bolan like the starship *Enterprise* cranking up its warp drive. The car bore straight down on the BMW and didn't look like it intended to move around him.

The car was about to run Bolan down as he approached the Masten Avenue overpass. Just as the car was about to make contact, the soldier veered off the road and jammed on the brakes, slowing as much as he could before the pavement ended. The Nissan rocketed past, but jammed on its brakes once the driver realized what Bolan had done.

When the pavement ended Bolan let off the brakes, stood up on the pegs, and rode the motorcycle up the embankment to Masten Avenue. At the top of the hill he rode across Masten and stopped at the embankment leading back down to the highway. The Nissan had skidded to a stop just past the overpass bridge and was starting to back up. The driver was too busy trying not to get hit by oncoming vehicles to look up and see Bolan standing above him. Bolan pulled his Desert Eagle from beneath his riding jacket. Taking aim at the steel roof, right about where he imagined the driver to be seated, he pumped an entire magazine through the sheet metal.

The Nissan accelerated hard and spun out of control, smashing into the cement bridge support between the northbound and southbound lanes. Bolan slammed a fresh magazine into the big hand cannon, reholstered it, and rode down the hill. Traffic had stopped behind the accident, and a small line of cars was forming toward the south. Pulling out his Desert Eagle, Bolan approached the car.

The driver was dead and the passenger wasn't doing much better. He hadn't been wearing a seat belt and when the car hit the cement pylon, he'd been slammed back into his seat with such force that he appeared to have broken his back. His SAR-21 still lay in his lap, but the man didn't appear to be able to move his arms. Both his right arm and the right arm of the driver bore the distinctive question-mark tattoo with which the soldier had become far too familiar over the past few days.

The passenger barely held on to consciousness.

"Who sent you?" Bolan asked.

"The Malaysian," the man said just before he sunk into unconsciousness, confirming the soldier's suspicions. Bolan felt the pulse in the man's neck. He doubted the man was going to make it.

He could hear sirens approaching in the distance. A delay would likely result in the deaths of hundreds of thousands of people, so Bolan was on his bike riding toward San Francisco before the first emergency vehicle came into sight. Bolan held his speed to a reasonable level until after he'd passed the last squad car responding to the accident, then poured it on. He felt relatively sure he wouldn't get stopped for speeding since just about every available unit in a ten-mile area seemed to have headed for the accident site.

IN SPITE OF HIS DIVERSION on the way to the city, Bolan arrived at the fish market on Grant Street just ten minutes later than he had promised Osborne on the phone. Not wanting any distractions from the job at hand, the soldier dismissed his tardiness with the one word every Californian understood: "Traffic."

"I've scouted the area," Osborne said, "and there seem to be just two main entrances to the upper level, one in back that seems to be the one everyone uses and one inside the convenience store. Plus there is a fire escape on each end of the building."

"I've got a blueprint of the floor plan," Bolan said, "but it's old; the layout might be completely different." Bolan pulled the floor plan that he'd printed from the file Kurtzman had sent him from his back pocket and unfolded it for Osborne to see.

"There's one big main room up there, along with a bathroom and the two landings here and here." Bolan pointed to the landings on the stairway. The landing in the back was really its own small room but the one coming up from the store was just large enough for the door to swing open.

"When you get to the top of the stairs, try to find some

cover and defend your position until you hear a flashbang go off. You know the drill on that, right?" Bolan knew that Osborne would have learned the procedure for dealing with a flashbang when he'd received his blacksuit training, but he wanted to be sure.

"Close your eyes, cover you ears and scream like a lunatic."

"When you hear the shooting stop on my end, you can expect the flashbang to go off within ten seconds. When the flashbang explodes, rush into the main room."

Bolan wished he had two more people to cover each fire escape, but he'd have to make do with just him and Osborne and try to keep one eye on the fire escapes. "I'll take the back door—you go up through the door in the store. Watch the store owner—it looks like he's dirty and he might try something. What are you packing?"

Osborne raised his jacket to reveal a Glock 26 in a Bianchi CarryLok high-ride belt holster. "Plus I brought this," he said. He pulled back his jacket on the other side to reveal a Glock with an extended 33-round magazine sticking out of the grip.

"Is that an 18?" the soldier asked, referring to Glock's full-auto 9 mm machine pistol, the Austrian company's version of the Beretta 93-R that the soldier carried.

"It's more of a 17-and-a-half," Osborne said. "It started life as a 17 and I did a little work to the trigger group."

Bolan knew the gun Osborne had brought was highly illegal and would net the former officer ten years in prison if he was caught carrying it. But Osborne, like Bolan, was operating outside the boundaries of any law, and his weapon was perfect for the job at hand. And that job entailed nothing short of saving more than one million lives.

"How many BNG bangers do you think are in there?" Bolan asked.

"I've seen at least ten men go in already this morning. I imagine there were a few who spent the night here. The department's been keeping an eye on this place and there are always at least three or four guys in there at all times. So what's the plan?"

"Go to the stairway inside the store. Give me thirty seconds, then kick the door down and come up the stairs. These guys are heavily armed, so when you first go in, shoot anything that isn't me. As soon as things settle down, get selective. We need to keep some of them alive to try to find out where they've hidden the nuclear device."

Bolan went to the rear entrance, watching the fire escape as he went. He glanced at his watch when he got to the door, then kicked down the door and stormed up the stairs. He saw the barrel of an SAR-21 come into sight over the half wall surrounding three sides of the stairwell. He aimed his .44 Magnum Desert Eagle at the wall, right about where the man holding the gun would be standing, and fired off three quick rounds. The report from the gun echoed through the building like an exploding gas main, followed by agonized screams from the other side of the flimsy half wall.

Two more men appeared at the top of the stairs. As soon as Bolan saw the tops of their heads appear over the top of the stairwell, he triggered a quick shot into each man. Both shots found their mark and punched through the skulls of the gangbangers. Their momentum carried the corpses over the edge of the stairwell and both bodies tumbled down the staircase, landing on the stoop beneath the smashed-in door. Bolan managed to step out of the way and avoid both men, but one of their falling rifles caught him across his back and knocked the wind out of him.

The soldier didn't let that slow him down and he continued up the stairs, watching and listening for more movement. The room at the top of the stairs sounded quiet, but he heard shots coming from the other end of the building. He heard the distinct sound of a 9 mm machine pistol, but he also heard the booming of rounds coming from a short-barreled rifle set to full-auto.

Bolan saw that the area at the top of the stairs was empty, but he could hear excited voices coming from the main room. He moved to the top of the stairs, reloading his gun on the way. Then, crouching just below the top step, he pulled the pin on a flashbang and lobbed it into the main room. He ducked down with his hands to his ears and let out a loud yell while the flashbang exploded.

The soldier rushed through the door and was in the room before the echoes of the blast had died down. He saw Osborne burst into the room at the opposite end. The people closest to him were completely incapacitated by the blast, but the men at the far end of the room recovered quickly and were raising SAR-21s to fire at Osborne.

Bolan had the Desert Eagle in his right hand and the Beretta in his left. He opened up with both guns and three men at the other end of the room fell to the floor. Osborne took out two more with the Glock. But there were four more men taking aim at him. Osborne dropped to the floor as rounds flew over his head.

The Executioner drew a bead on one of the gunman with his Desert Eagle and fired. The man's head disappeared in a red mist. At the same time he sprayed almost an entire magazine from the Beretta at the other three men, dropping two of them. Osborne took out the fourth man with his Glock, which locked open, empty, after the man fell.

Bolan covered Osborne with the Desert Eagle while he dropped one of the long stick magazines from the Glock and slammed home another thirty-three-rounder. He pressed the slide release, slamming a round into battery just as the Desert Eagle ran dry. Now it was Osborne's turn to cover the soldier while he reloaded. Several of the men who had been closest to the grenade had regained their senses and were raising their guns, but Osborne ran toward them with his Glock ready to spray the group and shouted, "Freeze!"

Two of the men stopped, but the man closest to Bolan continued to raise his gun, preparing to shoot the soldier who had just finished slapping fresh magazines into his pistols. Osborne fired at the man, opening up half a dozen holes in his chest. The man fell to the floor, dead.

Meanwhile Bolan had both of the two remaining BNG members in the sights of his guns. Both men raised their hands. Bolan walked up to them and asked, "Have any of you worked with bin Osman?"

The two men looked at each other as if one could somehow save the other's life. They assessed the situation and concluded that they couldn't. A dozen of their comrades lay strewn about the room, dead or dying. The pair realized that they were dealing with an unknown quantity. These men weren't cops; they were far too bloodthirsty and ruthless to be members of any law enforcement agency, and no cop carried weaponry like they packed. And they weren't members of any rival gang—they were too old and too white.

The gangbangers had no idea who these attackers were, but they could see that they were people best not messed with. Half of their gang had disappeared or been killed in the past several days and these two men seemed to have been responsible. They were the reason the entire gang had been called to the clubhouse that morning, or rather, what remained of the gang. When the big man asked again, they decided to cooperate.

"You mean the Malaysian?" one asked.

"Yes, the Malaysian."

"We don't know what he's doing," the other said. "We haven't seen him since yesterday."

"What did you do for him yesterday?"

"Nothing. He helped us get jobs as security guards. We only saw him yesterday when he came to our job site with the fat white man."

"Where was the job site?" Bolan asked. "What did they do there?"

Before they could answer, the bathroom door burst open and another gangbanger flew from the room, his finger pressing down on the trigger of his SAR-21. Both Bolan and Osborne ducked to avoid the wild spray, but the two gangbangers who were about to tell the Executioner where the bomb was located were too stunned to duck.

Bolan and Osborne fired on the man simultaneously, dropping him in a hail of gunfire, but not before he'd taken out both of his buddies.

The Executioner seldom lost hope, but when the two BNG members who were going to tell him where to find the bomb died, he nearly succumbed. Then he remembered something a crusty old army sergeant once told him. "When you think you can't go on any farther, boy, it's time to shit your pants, jump in and swim."

17

Atay saw the American standing by the door to the BNG clubhouse upstairs, looking at his watch. He thought he should go and chase the man away, but the man looked like a cop. Something big was going on, and Atay didn't like it.

He didn't like much about what had been happening since bin Osman had contacted him, seeking the assistance of the BNG for some project that the Malaysian hadn't been willing to discuss. The only reason that Atay had agreed to assist the arrogant businessman was because he had been ordered to do so by his cousin Gulay, who was the leader of one of the largest Bahala Na Gangs in the Philippines.

Atay founded the first Bahala Na Gang in San Francisco, and although he was no longer an active member—he was far too old—he acted as a sort of business manager for the gang. Gulay had ordered him to cooperate with the Malaysian, and the money had been good, but it hadn't been worth what happened to the gang. At least twenty members had been killed that he knew of, and at least that many had gone missing in the last several days. Now he was unable to contact the Malaysian or the Saudi who ran the Malaysian's racing team.

Not only had the partnership with bin Osman been devastating to the club, but Atay had begun to worry about what exactly the Malaysian was planning. He'd heard bits and pieces from the members who had worked with bin Osman, at least from those who survived, and he hadn't liked what he heard. Atay had begun to worry that whatever the Malaysian was up to, it wasn't good for him or for the BNG.

And now this man was in his store, standing by the door that led upstairs to the BNG clubhouse. The entire gang, or what remained of it, had gathered upstairs, preparing to go to the mattresses. They had been through wars with rival gangs over the years, but they'd never experienced a buzz saw ripping through their ranks like this. From what he'd heard, most, if not all, of the deaths had been the result of a one-man rampage. The man responsible was supposedly a big, dark-haired American masquerading as a sales rep. At least that wasn't the man in his store now; this man was a medium-height man with hair that was more gray than black. He looked like a cop.

Atay's heart pounded when he saw the man kick down the door and head upstairs. Then the shooting started. Atay was safely ensconced behind the bullet-resistant shield that surrounded the checkout counter and till, but he hid down below the counter anyway.

He listened as the shots were fired. Some sounded like they were coming from the stairway and others sounded like they were coming from the back of the building. Some were softer, more muffled pops; others were loud, as if they'd been shot from a rifle. Most of the shots seemed to be coming from fully automatic weapons, but they were interspersed by extremely loud booming shots coming from some sort of single-round firing weapon.

Atay guessed that at least half the shots were coming from the assault rifles that the Malaysian had imported from Singapore. Bin Osman had provided the weapons at no cost, along with ample ammunition, but Atay felt as uncomfortable about that situation as he felt about the rest of his dealings with the sneaky Malaysian. Atay liked his weapons old school, like the old Smith & Wesson he now held in his shaking hand.

The shooting stopped and the upstairs was relatively quiet. Then a few moments later, it started up again. This time it lasted only a few seconds, and when it was done, Atay heard no more shots. He left his safe booth and went to the door to the stairway. He heard nothing. He looked inside the stairway and saw a body sprawled out on the steps. It was Frankie, one of the newest members of the BNG. At the top of the steps he saw another body. He couldn't make out whose body it was, but he could tell it wasn't the graying cop he'd seen go up the steps.

He slowly climbed the steps, holding the revolver ahead of him with both hands, ready to fire if necessary. Just as he reached the top of the stairway, two men came through the door. Before his aging reflexes could react, the men had drawn their own weapons and ordered him to drop his. From where he stood near the top of the staircase, he could see multiple bodies piled on the floor in the clubhouse and decided to comply, but he didn't want to drop the gun. It was one of his prized possessions. He slowly lowered the gun to the ground, his finger off the trigger.

"Please," he said. "Let me set it down gently. It is very valuable."

BOLAN AND OSBORNE CHECKED the pulses of the two bangers they'd been questioning before their panicked comrade shot them down. Both men were dead, as was everyone else in the room except for the two blacksuits. "What are we going to do now?" Osborne asked.

"Let's go down to the store," Bolan said. "Did you see the owner down there on your way up here?"

"He was hunkered down behind the counter."

"He's tight with the BNG. Maybe he knows something. Let's go down and talk to him."

Bolan knew the old man was a long shot, but at that moment he might be all that stood between the people of San Francisco and nuclear annihilation.

The men raced for the stairs, but stopped at the top of the steps when they saw the old man who owned the store coming up, a blued-steel revolver in his hands.

"Drop it!" both men shouted in unison.

The man slowly lowered the gun to the ground, apparently unfazed by the multiple gun barrels pointed at his face.

"Please," he said. "Let me set it down gently. It is very valuable." When he had placed the gun on the steps, he raised his hands, interlocking his fingers on the top of his head. He knew the drill.

Bolan picked up the revolver. It really was valuable, a pristine Smith & Wesson Registered model, the very first issue of the original .357 Magnum made between 1935 and 1939, back when that was the most powerful handgun caliber. The craftsmanship of the gun, with its hand checkering on the back strap and hammer, was like nothing seen on a mass-produced handgun in decades. The guns were so exclusive back in the 1930s that each one came with a certificate of registration, which is why they were called "Registered" models. Bolan knew prices for those revolvers easily ran into the five-figure range. He took extra care when he placed the old man's prized possession in his waistband. The Filipino seemed to appreciate the Executioner's gentle treatment of the antique weapon.

Bolan motioned for the man to come upstairs. When he saw the carnage around the room, his eyes went wide. "I should have told Gulay to go fuck himself," the man said, mostly to himself.

Bolan made a mental note to have Kurtzman check out this Gulay character, provided he survived long enough to talk to do so. Time was running out.

The soldier had only hours to find the bomb and disarm it, and that would only happen if the old man knew where it was located.

"Listen to me, old man," Bolan said. "If you think what you see here is bad, you haven't seen anything yet. If you don't give me some answers, you, your store, your home, your family and everyone you know are going to be dead before the evening news comes on tonight."

"So," the old man said, "it really is a nuclear weapon."

"You know about the bomb?" Bolan asked.

"I suspected, from what the boys were saying after they came back yesterday. That son of a bitch Gulay."

"Came back from where?" Bolan asked.

The old man looked distracted. "Where is Gulay? He's in the Philippines, of course."

"No," the Executioner said. "You said 'when the boys came back.' Came back from where?"

"Oh…the CSAA Building."

Bolan looked at Osborne. "He means the old California State Automobile Association building. It's been empty for years. If they aren't able to sell it soon, they're going to demolish it."

"Is that where bin Osman placed the bomb?" Bolan asked the old man.

"I don't know," the old man said.

"Why were gang members returning from there?" Bolan asked.

"I arranged for them to get jobs as security guards in the old building. I did this under orders from the Malaysian."

"Was bin Osman there yesterday?"

"Yes, he arrived with a fat American. My boys said the American seemed to be in the middle of some sort of mental breakdown. He wept the entire time he was there."

"What did bin Osman do in the building," the soldier asked.

"My men weren't supposed to be in the area where they were working, but I had a couple of them keeping an eye on the Malaysian while he was there. I don't trust the man."

"What did they see?"

"The Malaysian had the American construct some sort of device. Both of them were wearing protective suits, the kind you see people wearing in nuclear power plants. They left some strange things behind, like a container that looks like it was designed to transport some sort of nuclear waste."

"That building must be thirty stories tall," Osborne said. "Where did they assemble the device?"

"There is a loading dock just below the main floor, accessible through the alley in the rear of the building," the old man said. "They assembled the device in the storage area behind the loading dock."

"Is it still there?" Bolan asked.

"Yes. If bin Osman had had it moved, my men would have reported it to me. You say it's a bomb?"

"It's a nuclear device with enough power to kill everyone in San Francisco and the surrounding area," Bolan said.

"That's what I feared. Can you stop it?"

"I'm going to try. Can you call your men and tell them I'm coming?"

"I can try, but cell phone reception is bad in the old building, especially down in the loading dock area."

"How many men are in the building?"

"At least three," the old man said. "But if you leave now and drive like demons, you will get there just as the day shift comes on. Then there will be six men."

"Call them and tell them we're coming," Bolan ordered. "Tell them not to try to stop us."

The man called several numbers, but got nothing but voice mail messages. Then he tried several more with similar luck. The old man left a message after each call, telling the men to work with the big soldier. "I can't get through to any of them. My guess is that the day shift is already at the site."

Bolan and Osborne holstered their weapons and started to trot toward the door, but the old man's voice stopped them.

"Gentlemen," he said. "If my boys put up a fight, you have no choice but to take them out, just as you did the boys upstairs." The Executioner nodded in agreement with the man. "If it comes to that, please, don't let them suffer."

"I won't," the Executioner promised.

"One last thing," the old man said. "Could you please leave my gun on the newspaper stand inside the door when you leave? And please, be careful. I've had it a very long time." Bolan set the gun down just before he ran out the door. "Good luck, gentlemen," the old man said as they left.

He knew he was sending the two men to destroy the last remnants of the gang that had been the most important part of his life up until this point, but now he was too tired to continue his involvement with such nonsense. The knowledge that his cousin and mentor back in the Philippines had casually condemned the entire San Francisco gang to death, along with everyone else in the city, angered him.

He felt sad thinking about all the boys who had died during the past several days, and sadder still thinking about what was soon to happen to the remaining boys. But that was nothing compared to the thought of what might happen if these men failed. The old man knew that the two men racing from his store were the only chance he and hundreds of thousands of other people had of surviving the rest of this day.

If I live until tomorrow, the old man thought, looking at the faded blue question mark tattooed on his forearm, I'm going to see a doctor about having this removed.

Bolan and Osborne ran out to where Bolan had parked his bike. Osborne's car was parked several blocks away.

"Bring your car over here," Bolan ordered Osborne. "We won't need to worry about over-penetration at the CSAA Building. I have a couple of rifles in my top box that we'll want to use."

Bolan grabbed one of the two P90s from his top box and slung it over his shoulder, then covered it up with his riding jacket. By the time Osborne pulled up, he'd already put on his helmet and gloves and had the bike idling by the curb. "Take this," he told Osborne, handing him the second P90. "You know the way, so I'll follow you. Drive fast, but try not to get stopped. We don't have time to get pulled over for speeding."

Bolan followed Osborne's Audi down Grant Avenue to Broadway Street, where he made a sharp left. The torque-laden V-8 engine roared as Osborne took the corner, but the car's advanced all-wheel-drive system bit into the tarmac and the car shot around the corner without any drama. To keep up, Bolan had to turn the corner with considerably more effort, breaking the rear tire loose and sliding like a dirt-track racer.

The Audi flew down Broadway until it reached the Broadway tunnel. Traffic was light, even for a Sunday morning, and once the Audi hit the tunnel, Osborne put his foot into the accelerator and was soon hitting triple-digit speeds. To keep up, Bolan had to keep the throttle pinned to its stop and tuck in behind the small windscreen. When they neared the mouth of the tunnel, Osborne slowed down to a still socially reprehensible seventy miles per hour. Even though that was nearly double the speed limit, it felt slow after the high-speed run through the tunnel.

Osborne didn't slow the Audi to anywhere near the speed limit until he neared Van Ness Boulevard. When he turned left onto Van Ness, he once again went so fast that he forced the Executioner to slide around the corner to keep up. Van Ness was wider than Broadway and even less crowded, and the pair set a street-racing record for covering the nearly thirty blocks between Broadway and the CSAA Building.

When they got to the CSAA building, Osborne slammed the Audi around the corner of Fell Street and drove down into the entrance to the loading dock, Bolan's BMW in tow. The soldier dismounted the bike and met Osborne as he emerged from the Audi's diver's seat.

"How are we supposed to get in?" Bolan asked.

"I suppose knocking at the front door would be too easy," Osborne offered.

"I think that submachine gun hanging around your neck might be a little off-putting."

Bolan surveyed the situation. The entrance to the loading dock was in the southeast corner of the building, fairly well hidden from traffic on Fell Street.

"I don't think we have time to be subtle," the soldier said, producing several chunks of C-4 from a kit in the left saddlebag of his motorcycle.

There were two large overhead doors in the bay, along

with a pair of hinged steel doors that swung outward into the loading-dock area. Bolan molded one piece of the explosive around each of the four large hinges that held the steel doors in place and placed a blasting cap in each chunk. He motioned for Osborne to follow him to a nearby Dumpster. Once they were both crouched behind the Dumpster and holding their ears, Bolan hit the red button on a remote device that looked like a typical key fob for a car. The C-4 detonated. When the smoke cleared, the two doors had fallen from their hinges and lay across the loading dock.

THE YOUNG FILIPINO-AMERICAN MAN curled the cigarette paper into a trough and crumbled some of the sticky marijuana bud into the paper. With one practiced motion he rolled the paper into a perfectly cylindrical cigarette. He carefully licked the tip of his tongue across the glue strip on the top of the paper and finished rolling the cigarette. When he was finished, he placed the pointier end of the cigarette between his lips, took out a disposable lighter, and fired up the opposite end. When the paper caught fire he pulled as much smoke as possible into his lungs and held it while he passed the cigarette to his left.

The six BNG members, three of whom were getting off of their shifts guarding the CSAA building and three of whom were about to start their shifts, had developed a shift-changing ritual that involved passing around a joint or two along with several bottles of malt liquor. Normally it was the most pleasant part of their day, but the events of the last few days had them all terrified. Rather than simple diversion, they now used the alcohol and drugs to provide the courage they found they lacked when confronting this faceless monster who had decimated their ranks.

"Man, I need to chill out," the man who'd just rolled the

joint said. "All the shit that's been happening, that big motherfucker who's been capping everyone's ass, I'm about to lose my fucking mind."

"Get the fuck out of here," another said. "That's bullshit. Ain't no motherfucker like that. They've just bugged out somewhere for the weekend. They're just too goddamned lazy to work."

"No man," said a third. "They're dead. I saw Jake and them in Jake's Hummer, an' they're dead. Jake's mamma's already planned the funeral. They was supposed to bust a cap up some biker's ass and he busted caps up their asses instead."

"Get the fuck out of here," the other man repeated. "Ain't no man who can do all the shit they say this big guy is supposed to have done."

"I'm not shitting you, man. T.J. was there in Santa Cruz the night the big motherfucker killed just about everyone in a warehouse," another man said after he'd exhaled the marijuana smoke he'd been holding in his lungs while the other men conversed. "Motherfucker came out of nowhere and blew the place to shit. Killed everyone but T.J."

"What he's saying is true," another gangbanger said. "He's the same motherfucker who killed every one of our boys down in Davenport. Ain't none of us left but maybe fifteen, twenty boys."

"T.J. says the man's seven feet tall," one BNG banger said. "Motherfucker got guns coming out of his arms like Edward Scissorhands. Ain't no one can stop him because the motherfucker's dead already. He's one of them walking dead."

"I don't know about that zombie shit," yet another of the

group said. "But I hear he likes to cut people, slice their throats ear to ear. He's carving guts out while they're still alive."

"Shit," said the skeptic. "You all been to too many movies. Ain't no man can do any of that. You're all afraid of the boogeyman." Before he finished his thought a loud roar came from the loading dock area.

"What the fuck?" he asked.

"Man, someone's trying to get in through the loading docks," another said. "Where're your guns? Grab them motherfuckers and get out there!"

BOLAN AND OSBORNE were in the building and had taken defensive positions behind two garbage Dumpsters when the gang members came bursting into the storage area through a basement door. Each man carried an SAR-21. As the store owner had predicted, there were six of them. When they saw the blown door, they spread out, keeping behind cover as best they could. One chose a spot that protected him from Osborne's position, but left him wide open to Bolan. The soldier took the opportunity to open up on him with the P90, stitching him from the thigh up to his armpit. The man dropped the SAR-21 and fell to the ground, clutching his side.

At the same time, Osborne got off a shot at another of the attackers, punching a 5.7 mm round clean through his torso, right below his neck. Bolan could see that the shot had hit the man in his spine, and he watched the unfortunate gangbanger drop instantly.

So far none of the BNG members had even fired a shot. The remaining four men cowered together behind a forklift. Each held an assault rifle, but none of the men showed interest in firing their weapons. Bolan decided to try to get them to surrender.

"Drop your weapons!" the Executioner shouted. "Give yourself up and you won't die."

Bolan could hear the men talking among themselves.

"How do we know we can believe you?" one shouted. "You killed all of our brothers, man. Why wouldn't you kill us?"

"You have my word," the Executioner said. "You surrender, I promise we won't kill you. You don't surrender, I promise we kill you. That shouldn't be a tough decision."

"You won't kill us," the man said, "but you'll send us to jail for the rest of our lives. No thanks, man. I rather be dead."

"We won't even send you to jail if you help us find the bomb," Bolan said.

"What bomb?" another man asked.

"The one that the Malaysian set up in this building yesterday," the Executioner replied.

"What kind of bomb?" the man asked.

"The nuclear kind. It's set to go off this evening and when it does, it'll take all of San Francisco and most of Oakland with it. That includes you."

"Is that why the fat man wore the big rubber suit when he worked here yesterday?" the man asked.

Bolan thought he must be referring to an NBC suit. "That's why. Your boss bin Osman was trying to kill you guys along with everyone else."

"I'll kill that motherfucker," the man said.

"Too late," the Executioner said. "He's dead. What do you say? You help us and live or fight us and die?"

The gangbangers talked among themselves for a few moments before one said, "We're throwing down. Don't shoot, man."

One by one the Filipinos tossed their SAR-21s to the floor

and came out with their hands up, their fingers interlocked over their heads.

"Check them for other weapons," Bolan told Osborne.

The blacksuit found at least one knife on each of them and one of them had a handgun stuck in the waistband of his pants. When they were clean of weapons, the Executioner said, "Okay, now show us the bomb."

BOLAN KNEW HE WAS IN TROUBLE when he examined the explosive device. It differed radically from the schematic drawings he'd pulled from Gunthar Maurstad's corpse and the instructions he'd received from Kurtzman didn't match up with what he saw before him. Kurtzman had a team of experts on standby to help talk him through disabling the device, but he had no cell phone signal in the underground storage area covered by thirty stories of steel and concrete.

A digital timer on the device indicated that it would explode in a little over six hours. Bolan sketched out a schematic of the wiring he saw on the device and went outside to call Kurtzman.

Kurtzman patched him into a conference call with the group of explosive experts that Hal Brognola had assembled to assist the Executioner in dismantling the device.

"It sounds like Maurstad had to deviate from his original plan at the last minute," Tom Gardiner, one of the team members, said, and the others concurred. "My guess is that he had to rig some sort of off-the-shelf clock to the detonator and was forced to improvise."

The men had copies of Maurstad's original drawings, and Bolan described the changes he'd seen on the actual device.

"This isn't good," Gregory Lefrooth, one of the other team members, said. "I think I know what he did." Lefrooth explained his theory to the others and they agreed that his hypothesis was almost certainly correct.

"This could be disabled by clipping a single wire. The trouble is that there's no way for us to tell which wire it is. The only way would be to dismantle the device, but that would risk detonation."

"It doesn't sound like a very stable setup," Gardiner interjected. "I think upsetting the detonator would almost certainly set off the bomb."

The others agreed.

"It sounds like clipping a wire is the clear way to go," Bolan said. "So how do I decide which wire it is?"

"From what you describe," Gardiner said, "I don't think Maurstad set the bomb up to detonate if you clip the wrong wire."

"So I can just start cutting wires until the clock quits counting down?" Bolan asked.

"I don't think it will be that easy. I believe that cutting the wires might affect the rate of the countdown. Cut the wrong wire, and six hours could become six minutes. Or six seconds."

"Couldn't I just disable the timer?" Bolan asked.

"You could, but that won't stop the detonator. The timer is just there to provide information; it doesn't control anything. The only thing you'll accomplish by disabling the timer would be to prevent you from knowing when the bomb was going to explode."

"So I'm going to have to start cutting wires and hope for the best."

"That looks like it's your only option," Gardiner said.

BOLAN CROUCHED over the device with wire cutters in hand. He estimated how long it would take him to cut all the wires should he clip the wrong one first and speed up the detonation process. The fact that the device was fairly large—the tubular object stood almost four feet high and was about thirty inches in diameter at its widest point—and that the wires were not located in one spot but ran in and out of the complex device in what appeared to be a haphazard fashion, conspired to slow down his reaction time. In his mind he plotted out an order for cutting the wires that seemed most possible to do in less than six seconds.

With one eye on the timer, he cut the first wire, ready to start cutting the rest as fast as he could should the timer speed up. It didn't speed up, but neither did it stop counting down. He moved to the next wire, again mentally preparing himself for the mad dash of cutting all the wires in under six seconds should he clip the wrong wire.

When Bolan clipped the next wire, the countdown on the timer switched from five hours, seventeen minutes, and twenty-six seconds to five minutes and seventeen seconds. Bolan still had seven wires to cut, but even though this last cut hadn't worked out as planned, he continued in the same sequence he'd mapped out in his head. It was the only way he would be able to cut the remaining six wires in the allotted time should the minutes switch to seconds.

Bolan cut the next wire in his sequence and nothing happened, but the wire after that tripped the sequence from minutes to seconds. The soldier switched into his alternative plan without hesitation. His life had depended on his timing ever since he'd begun his war and he'd developed a mental clock that was as reliable as a metronome. He clipped the first, the second, and the third wires in less than three seconds, but the fourth was around the far side of the device. With his mental clock keeping pace with the timer, he reached around and clipped the final wire.

The timer stopped.

His mental clock told him that he had less than fractions of a second to spare before the device detonated. Mack Bolan had perhaps the strongest nerves of any man who had ever walked the Earth, but coming this close to being on top of an exploding nuclear bomb had shaken him. It wasn't his own mortality that had rattled his nerves; it was the fact that he'd come so close to letting down his country and bringing about the deaths of hundreds of thousands—perhaps millions—of people. The soldier took a deep breath and looked at the timer. He'd stopped the countdown with just twenty-three one hundredths of a second left before detonation.

Bolan realized he was drenched with sweat. It was hot in the storage area behind the loading docks, but the soldier knew that wasn't the reason for the sweat. He looked around at the other men in the room. Osborne and the four surviving members of the BNG were as drenched with sweat as he was. The five men stared at him, their eyes wide, their jaws hanging slack, as if trying to speak, but no one said a word.

After an uncomfortably long time, Osborne broke the silence.

"You did it?" he asked.

"We did it," Bolan replied.

"What about those four?" Osborne asked.

"I told them they're free to go, so they're free to go."

The Executioner looked at the four men. "This doesn't mean my friend here won't come after you the next time you break the law," he told them. "You've seen what he's like when he's mad. Now get out of here before I change my mind."

When they'd left, Bolan walked out to the loading bay and called Kurtzman to have him send in a team to dispose of the device.

Epilogue

Eddie Anderson got a good start off the pole position and rode one of the best races of his life. The only person who could run with him was his teammate, Daniel Asnorossa, but he never got within three seconds of Anderson.

He was riding the race of his life, but he couldn't shake the thought of his brother Darrick from his head, so he decided to go with it and imagined he was following Darrick. Eddie had watched Darrick race this track dozens of times, and he'd memorized every line his older brother had ever taken through every corner, but he'd never been able to put together the perfect lap here quite like Darrick could. Now, in his imagination, he was watching Darrick take the absolute perfect line. Eddie poured on the gas and was running well ahead of the pace of everyone but Asnorossa, but he wasn't going fast enough to catch the image of his brother that he imagined in his head.

Darrick's team had pulled out of the race entirely. The discovery of the bodies in the Team Free Flow garage had created incredible turmoil in the paddock, and there had even been talk of canceling the race. Ultimately the promoters decided to go on with the event, figuring that the body count might rise significantly if they tried to turn back tens of thousands of rabid fans on race day. They figured the crowd would be especially incensed once they learned the reason for the cancellation had been because of a tragedy that had befallen a third-rate back marker team that absolutely no one cared about after the death of its star rider, Darrick Anderson.

No one really cared about Team Free Flow, but Darrick's name still meant something to the crowd, and Eddie had noted hundreds of people wearing T-shirts with images of Darrick from Darrick's winning years. Many even carried banners with Darrick's name on them.

But even more carried banners with Eddie's name on them, and for every T-shirt with Darrick's image, there were three with Eddie's. But the Darrick banners were all that mattered to Eddie. He was riding for his brother as much as he was riding for himself and his team. And he was riding extremely well. He passed his pit board, which told him that Asnorossa had fallen to four seconds behind him.

In his mind he was chasing his brother, who seemed to disappear into the heat waves shimmering up off the hot asphalt. Eddie was riding right on the edge of his tire-performance envelope, and even though he knew better than to risk losing the front end and crashing, costing him valuable points and perhaps ultimately the championship, he pushed his bike even harder trying to catch up with his imagined sibling.

In his mind, Eddie noticed his brother was taking slightly different lines through the corners than he'd remembered him taking. Eddie followed these imagined lines, which were unorthodox, but they worked. He apexed a bit earlier in some corners and a bit later in others, deviating from the accepted fast line through Laguna Seca, but there was a method to his madness. Eddie began to adopt the lines he imagined his brother taking and he started to shave time off his laps. After putting together several laps with the new lines, he passed his pit board to see that he'd just set a new lap record, and not just the lap record for race times—he'd set an all-time lap record, beating his qualifying record set the previous day by nearly half a second.

Eddie knew he had more in him and his bike. He continued to follow the strange lines he imagined his brother taking and his lap times continued to drop. Four laps before the race was over, he set his fastest lap, beating his record of the previous day by over a second.

Asnorossa still hung with him until his fastest lap, falling back only five seconds by the time Eddie set the record. But on that incredible lap, Asnorossa pushed it too hard and he went off the track in Rainey Curve, exactly where Eddie had gone off in practice. Asnorossa almost made it back on track but dropped the bike in the kitty litter just off the edge of the asphalt. He got the bike back up before it stalled and got back on track. The pair of Ducatis had built up such an amazing lead over the third-place rider that Asnorossa was eventually able to bring his bike in at second place, despite his off-track adventure.

Meanwhile Eddie kept up his blistering pace, but he still couldn't catch his imagined riding companion. He was still going faster than anyone ever had before, and on the final lap Eddie wheelied past the finish line, taking the checkered flag.

The crowd lost its collective mind. In his imagination, Eddie saw Darrick turn around and flash him a V-for-victory sign.